A dangerous field trip . . .

Elizabeth gasped. Inside the passenger room of the Island Dreamer *were two men, all tied up! One man was wearing a white captain's uniform, and the other was in navy blue work clothes. They were both unconscious, and the crewman's forehead had a thin trickle of blood on it.*

Elizabeth felt her heart start to pound. What could this mean? Suddenly her uneasiness about the field trip rose up inside her again—only much more sharply than before. As Elizabeth and her friends stood there, frozen, the man in the white uniform opened his eyes groggily and blinked at them. "Did you hear me knocking?" he asked weakly.

"Yes," Jessica whispered, staring at him.

Elizabeth swallowed hard. "Who—who are you?" she asked, trying to sound brave. "What happened here?"

"I'm Captain Thomas Moreland," the man said, his words a little slurred. "I own the Island Dreamer. *This is my crewman, Walt Lufkin. We've been hijacked."*

SWEET VALLEY TWINS

Deadly Voyage

Written by
Jamie Suzanne

Created by
FRANCINE PASCAL

BANTAM BOOKS
NEW YORK · TORONTO · LONDON · SYDNEY · AUCKLAND

DEADLY VOYAGE
A BANTAM BOOK : 0 553 50313 8

Originally published in USA by Bantam Books

First publication in Great Britain

PRINTING HISTORY
Bantam edition published 1996

The trademarks "Sweet Valley" and "Sweet Valley Twins"
are owned by Francine Pascal and are used under license by
Bantam Books and Transworld Publishers Ltd.

Conceived by Francine Pascal.

Produced by Daniel Weiss Associates, Inc.,
33 West 17th Street, New York, NY 10011

Copyright © 1995 by Francine Pascal

Cover photo by Oliver Hunter

Bantam Books are published by Transworld Publishers Ltd,
61–63 Uxbridge Road, Ealing, London W5 5SA,
in Australia by Transworld Publishers (Australia) Pty Ltd,
15-25 Helles Avenue, Moorebank, NSW 2170,
and in New Zealand by Transworld Publishers (NZ) Ltd,
3 William Pickering Drive, Albany, Auckland.

Printed and bound in Great Britain by
Cox & Wyman Ltd, Reading, Berkshire.

To Judy and Alan Adler

One

"Elizabeth! Elizabeth!"

Elizabeth Wakefield tried to ignore the insistent tugging on her shoulder. Shutting her eyes more tightly, she snuggled deeper under the covers. After all, it was Saturday.

"Elizabeth!" Someone started bouncing annoyingly on her bed. Elizabeth gritted her teeth and buried her face in her pillow.

"Fine, then," said the voice. "You stay here. I'll go on the field trip alone. And since you're not going, you won't mind if I borrow your scuba fins."

Elizabeth's eyes popped open, and she sat up so fast she almost knocked Jessica onto the floor. "Oh, my gosh!" she exclaimed. "The field trip! Quick, what time is it?" She squinted blearily at the clock on her bedside table.

"Seven o'clock on the dot," Jessica replied. "*I've* been up for ages. You better hurry up and get dressed."

Brushing her long blond hair out of her eyes, Elizabeth looked at Jessica suspiciously. "You got up early on a Saturday?" She frowned. "Who are you, and what have you done with the real Jessica?"

"Elizabeth, don't try to be funny," Jessica complained. "It's too early in the morning for that. You know I'm up early to get ready for the big field trip. Now, get out of bed, already, and tell me where your scuba fins are."

Elizabeth felt a rush of excitement. Today was the day she and Jessica had been looking forward to for weeks: selected sixth-, seventh-, and eighth-grade students from Sweet Valley Middle School were going on an all-day field trip to Santa Maria Island, about an hour and a half away by boat. There they would spend the day observing wildlife and exploring the natural, unspoiled beauty of an uninhabited coastal island. Not only would it be a lot of fun, but the students who participated would get extra credit in science class.

"What's wrong with your own fins?" Elizabeth asked, swinging her legs out of bed and shuffling to the bathroom that connected her bedroom and Jessica's.

"They clash with my new bikini," Jessica answered, her voice muffled because she was pawing through the bottom of Elizabeth's closet. "Yours have that streak of neon purple on them."

Rolling her eyes, Elizabeth turned on the water in the sink and started brushing her teeth. She *could* tell Jessica no. She *could* tell Jessica to get out of her closet. But it wouldn't do any good. Her twin sister was a force of nature, kind of like a small, cheerful hurricane. It was usually best—and always easiest—just to give in.

In the mirror, Jessica appeared behind Elizabeth, triumphantly holding up Elizabeth's scuba fins. After tossing them into her own room, Jessica came back and started brushing her hair, nudging Elizabeth out of the way.

Sometimes it was hard to believe they were identical twins, Elizabeth mused as she washed her face. True, they were both twelve years old and in sixth grade at Sweet Valley Middle School. They both had long blond hair, blue-green eyes, and a dimple in their left cheek. But that was where the similarities ended. All anyone had to do was look at their two bedrooms to see that they were completely different people. Jessica's bedroom was always a total disaster area. Elizabeth couldn't remember the last time she had actually seen Jessica's floor. It, like every other surface in her room, was covered with piles of clothes, books, tapes and CDs, hair accessories, magazines, ancient schoolwork, and even used plates and drinking glasses. Not to mention any item of Elizabeth's that

Jessica had "borrowed" and had either lost or not returned yet. Frankly, being in Jessica's room made Elizabeth feel twitchy. How her sister studied in there was a complete mystery.

Not that studying was Jessica's priority. She lived for fashion, gossip, boys, and her friends in the Unicorn Club, a group of girls who considered themselves the prettiest and most popular in Sweet Valley Middle School.

Elizabeth, on the other hand, was much more serious and studious, and her own room was a perfect match for her. It was neat and tidy, easy to work in and restful to relax in. Leaving the bathroom, Elizabeth surveyed her room with pride. Her schoolbooks were stacked on her desk, all her clothes were put away, everything was in its place. At any moment she could find anything she needed: books, clothes, CDs. Just the way she liked it.

Jessica breezed back into the room as Elizabeth was getting dressed. "What do you think?" she asked, striking a pose. "Tie the T-shirt in a knot at my waist, or let it hang down in a more casual look?"

"Um, gee, Jess, I don't know," Elizabeth said. "I mean, it's such an earth-shattering question—I don't want to rush into an answer."

Jessica sighed. "Someday you'll take fashion seriously," she said loftily. "What swimsuit are you wearing?"

Elizabeth pulled up her sleeveless T-shirt and showed Jessica the flowered blue-and-green tank suit she had on under her clothes. "What about you?" she asked.

"My brand-new purple bikini," Jessica said, wiggling her eyebrows suggestively. "The one with the unicorn appliqué. Wait till the other Unicorns see it—they're going to die." She looked very pleased at the prospect.

Elizabeth grinned and shook her head a little. The Unicorns weren't really her favorite people. Privately, she thought of them as the Snob Squad. She and her own best friends, Amy Sutton and Maria Slater, had never been interested in being Unicorn Club members. But Jessica loved being a Unicorn and took her club duties—like the one about wearing something purple, the color of royalty, every day—very seriously.

"Why don't you wear your red two-piece?" Jessica suggested, sliding her ponytail through a white baseball cap. "So you can work on your tan."

"We're going to be studying sea mammals, and birds, and plants," Elizabeth reminded her. "We won't have time to work on our tans. This is supposed to be a science field trip, remember?"

Jessica shrugged. "All I know is, we're going to be on a boat, then on an island with a beach, then on a boat again. If this isn't a tanning opportunity, I don't know what is."

Before Elizabeth could respond, there was a knock on her door, and Alice Wakefield stuck her head into the room. "Are you two about ready?"

she asked. "We have to get going—the boat is leaving promptly at eight o'clock."

"We're ready, Mom," Elizabeth said, gathering a couple of notebooks and pens and stuffing them into a waterproof backpack. As editor of the sixth-grade school newspaper, *The Sweet Valley Sixers*, Elizabeth was planning to write a big three-part article about their field-trip experience. She felt another flutter of anticipation as she and Jessica pounded downstairs in their sneakers. Today was going to be an unforgettable day—she could feel it.

"Wait, Mom!" Jessica cried as her mother opened the passenger door of the Wakefields' minivan.

"What?" her mother asked. "Did you forget something?"

"I don't know," Jessica said, looking worried. "Let me just check." Quickly she opened her large duffel bag and began rooting around inside. "Extra lip gloss, mousse, tanning lotion . . ."

"Jessica, come on," Elizabeth said. "Just get in the car. I don't want to be late."

"Jessica, we really have to leave now," Mrs. Wakefield said, tapping her foot against the cement. "The boat won't wait for us."

"Sure it will," Jessica said confidently, zipping her bag up. She clambered into the backseat of the minivan, and Elizabeth climbed in after her. Their mother shut the door with a bang, then got into the front seat and started the engine. "After all, you're one of the parent chaperons. Not only that, but they'll have to wait for all of the Unicorns."

"What do you mean?" Elizabeth asked as the minivan pulled out into the street. "Are all the Unicorns planning to be fashionably late?"

"No," Jessica said, bouncing in her seat. "No later than us, anyway. I mean, you *know* we have to pick them all up. That's why I kept trying to hurry you up this morning."

"What!" Mrs. Wakefield cried, staring at Jessica in the rearview mirror.

"Yeah. Mom, don't you remember?" Jessica said patiently. "I told you I'd promised them all a ride. Well, not really *all* of them. Just Lila, Mandy, Janet, and Ellen."

"Oh, Jessica," Elizabeth moaned. "We're going to be totally late!"

"No, no, they're all on the way," Jessica said firmly, not meeting her mother's eyes. "Besides, what's the big deal if we're a minute or two late?" It was just this kind of unnecessary nitpickiness that Jessica refused to give in to. People had to be more flexible, in her opinion.

"Actually, it *is* kind of a big deal, Jessica," Mrs. Wakefield said, sounding irritated. "The boat has to leave right on time because we have to return home right on time."

"OK, OK, so we need to get there on time," Jessica said. "I got it. But it'll be fine, you'll see. I'm sure no one will mind if we get back a teensy bit late tonight."

"It's not just that," Mrs. Wakefield said, taking the turn to Lila's house. "Apparently, the weather will be beautiful all day until late afternoon, but we're expecting a nasty storm then. It's important that the boat get back before dinnertime, so we don't get caught in it."

Looking out the car window, Jessica saw nothing but pure, cloudless blue sky. It was completely impossible that a storm could be brewing somewhere. She guessed some TV weatherperson was overreacting to some satellite picture somewhere. *Typical*.

"I wish you had mentioned giving everyone rides earlier," Mrs. Wakefield continued, stopping in front of Lila's huge mansion and honking the horn. "You should have asked me, honey."

"I did," Jessica insisted in a small voice. In the backseat, she slunk down a little, still looking out the window. It was amazing how people got upset about the least little things. She noticed this all the time.

"Did you bring the new Johnny Buck tape?" Janet Howell asked Lila Fowler. Janet was an eighth-grader, as well as the president of the Unicorns *and* the head Booster. The Boosters were Sweet Valley Middle School's cheerleading squad. All the Unicorns were also Boosters, but there were a couple of non-Unicorn Boosters—Amy Sutton and Winston Egbert.

"*Bucking the System*? Of course," Lila said

smugly, sitting back against the minivan bench seat. Lila Fowler was Jessica's best friend, after Elizabeth. Her parents were divorced, and she lived with her father, who was one of the richest people in Sweet Valley. "Not only that, but last night Daddy brought home Melody Power's latest album, too. I have it right here," she said, patting her leather tote bag. *"Power to the People."*

"That hasn't been released in America yet," Mandy Miller said with wide eyes.

"I know," Lila said, tossing her long, brown hair over one shoulder. "It's a European import. I haven't even listened to it yet. Daddy said he got it in London, at this cool record shop."

"This is going to be so great," Jessica said, bouncing happily next to Elizabeth. "There is just no way this day won't be perfect."

"I can't wait to see some of the sea lions and otters," Elizabeth joined in. "I just wish it was the right season for gray whales. But they won't be here until winter."

For a long moment, all five Unicorns stared silently at Elizabeth.

"Gray whales," Janet repeated, giving Jessica a sympathetic look.

Elizabeth knew what that look meant. The Unicorns felt sorry for Jessica for having such a boring sister. She remembered when Jessica had been trying to get her to join the Unicorns—she had actually attended a few meetings, and she'd had about as much fun as going to the dentist. If she had joined, she would probably be completely brain-dead by now. *Oh, well,* she thought with a private smile, leaning her head against the window. She and Jessica had different interests, but they would still always be best friends.

"Wait till you guys see my new bikini," Jessica said in the awkward silence. "Guess what color it is."

"Royal purple?" Ellen Riteman guessed.

"Yep," Jessica said happily. "It's totally cool. I got it at the mall last weekend."

"Look! There's the marina," Mandy said, pressing her nose against the window. "Wow! How many kids are coming today?"

"I think about twenty-four, maybe twenty-five or so, all in all," Mrs. Wakefield answered, pulling the minivan into a parking space. "I have to go over the list with Mr. Seigel." Mr. Seigel was Elizabeth's science teacher, and he had organized today's trip.

"Sun, sand, and water, here we come!" Jessica exclaimed. She faced Elizabeth. "Ready for the best field trip ever?"

"Ready!" Elizabeth replied, smiling back.

Two

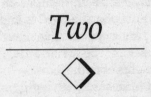

"Hey, Elizabeth!"

Elizabeth turned to see Maria Slater waving at her from the big cement dock where she was standing with Amy Sutton and Todd Wilkins. Grabbing her duffel, she headed toward her friends.

"I thought you'd never get here," Amy said, adjusting her sunglasses on her nose.

"I thought I never would either," Elizabeth said dryly. "At the last minute, Jessica told Mom that she'd promised rides to half the Unicorns."

Maria laughed. "It's funny that they're even coming on this trip. Don't they know it means extra credit in science class?"

"I think they just want the chance to explore a new beach," Elizabeth told her with a grin. "The only thing Jessica was regretting is that we're not actually missing a school day for this. But I can't wait to see all the stuff at Santa Maria Island."

"Me too," Todd said. In the past couple of months, he and Elizabeth had become sort of boyfriend and girlfriend. Today Elizabeth thought he looked really cute in fluorescent jams down to his knees and a black T-shirt with the arms cut off. "I've never seen elephant seals up close before," he continued. "Sometimes the males get into fights over the females."

"Typical," Maria said with a giggle. "I can't wait to see some of the plants—they're supposed to be totally cool. I heard there was a kind of flower there that doesn't appear anywhere else in the world." Then her eyes focused on something behind Elizabeth. "Oh, my gosh, what's Randy got?"

Turning, Elizabeth saw Randy Mason, the boy genius and science nerd of the sixth grade, lugging a big cardboard box. The top was open, and they could see metal antennas and wires and coils sticking up out of it.

"Hi," he said, puffing up to them. After putting the box down gently, he wiped his brow and pushed his glasses up on his nose.

"What is all that, Randy?" Amy asked.

"Science equipment," he explained. "I'm going to run some tests while we're out on the boat. Weather stuff, wind currents, directional sonar findings."

"You're like Mr. Seigel's dream come true," Maria marveled.

Randy blushed. "Yeah, well," he muttered.

"Amy and I are going to cover this field trip for the *Sixers*," Elizabeth said. Amy worked on the sixth-grade newspaper with Elizabeth. "I'd like to talk to you about your experiment results, when you get them."

"Sure," Randy said shyly, brushing his hair off of his forehead.

"This boat looks pretty neat, huh?" Maria gestured to the mid-size, white-painted vessel tied to the dock next to them. It was wide and flat, kind of like a cross between a small tugboat and a ferry, and was called the *Island Dreamer*. There was a large room right in the middle of the deck, and then a pilothouse that stood up a little taller. Elizabeth knew the pilothouse was where the captain steered the boat. In both the front and the back were large open decks made of polished wood that gleamed in the sunshine.

"Yeah," Elizabeth agreed, jotting down a few descriptive notes in her notebook. "When can we go on?"

Shading her eyes, Maria looked back down the dock. "Anytime, I guess. Looks like just about everyone's here. There's my dad and your mom, looking at a clipboard with Mr. Seigel."

"Probably checking off names," Todd guessed. "They know all of *us* are here. I say we go on board."

"Good idea," Amy said. "The gangplank's down. Let's go grab some good seats."

After a last look back at where her mom was

trying to organize things with Mr. Slater and Mr. Seigel, Elizabeth nodded. "We might as well," she said. "Or else all the Unicorns will crowd us into a corner."

"Yo! Jer! Wait up," Bruce Patman said.

Jessica and the rest of the Unicorns watched as Bruce jogged up to Jerry McAllister. Bruce had a huge duffel bag slapping against his side, and he and Jerry hit high fives.

"What's he got in there?" Janet asked. "Half his wardrobe?"

"You've got a huge duffel yourself," Jessica pointed out, unwrapping a stick of gum.

Janet glared at her. "It just so happens that I have important Unicorn stuff in here—like the latest copy of *Teen Dream* magazine, featuring Johnny Buck. And other cool stuff. But if you're not interested . . ."

"No, no, I didn't say that," Jessica answered quickly. "I'm sure whatever you have in your duffel is much more important than anything he has. And I guess his bag *is* bigger. It just didn't look like it. At first. You know." Jessica gave Janet an apologetic grin. Janet was just about the most popular girl at Sweet Valley Middle School, and she didn't like people—especially Unicorns—to forget that fact.

"I have to say," Belinda Layton said in a low voice, "that Bruce looks pretty cute in his surfing jams."

"Yeah." Jessica examined him critically. He and

Jerry were now leaning against the side rail, looking out at the ocean. "Some boys would look like total geeks in them, but Bruce can carry them off."

Tamara Chase nodded her agreement. "But it's practically criminal to waste so much cuteness on him when he's so stuck on himself and snobby."

"He sort of has a right to be snobby," Janet said, defending him. "He's cute, he's rich, he has a great house, he's on the basketball team . . ."

"That doesn't mean he should be snobby," Belinda objected.

"Maybe he'll grow out of it," Ellen Riteman suggested hopefully. "Like, by high school."

"So where is this tub we're going on?" Bruce was asking loudly. Jerry pointed to the *Island Dreamer*, and the two boys laughed. "What a dump," Bruce said. "My dad's cabin cruiser is fifty times better than that."

Lila smirked. "I've seen his dad's cabin cruiser," she whispered knowingly, "and let me tell you, it's not like it's the *Queen Elizabeth* or anything. I mean, it's *nothing* compared with my dad's big new sailboat. The one that sleeps ten."

Jessica rolled her eyes. Lila and Bruce had lots in common, now that she thought of it. They *both* liked to brag about how privileged they were. Lila especially liked to show off in front of Jessica.

"Hey, look," Janet said, pointing. "They've started loading the food."

Aaron Dallas, Ken Matthews, and Donald Zwerdling were helping to carry several ice chests down the gangplank to the boat. Everyone going on the field trip had been split into groups, and each group had contributed some kind of food. Jessica and the Unicorns had made some of Jessica's famous, prizewinning JEM cookies, from the recipe she had developed for *Lifestyles of the French and Famous*, her favorite television show. The J in JEM stood for Jessica. The E stood for Elizabeth, because it was Elizabeth's plan that had saved Jessica during the whole cookie fiasco. And the M was the W in Wakefield turned upside down. Elizabeth and Winston Egbert, the class clown, had been responsible for several large bottles of soda. Todd Wilkins and Ken Matthews had brought bags of chips, Amy and Maria had been assigned fruit, and Randy, Donald, and Jerry had gotten sandwiches from the Valley Deli.

"A bunch of kids are already on board," Jessica said. "Maybe we should get on, too."

"Just a minute, girls," Mr. Seigel said, coming up behind them. "Let me just check you off our list." Quickly, he matched each Unicorn with a name on his clipboard, then nodded. "OK, you guys can get on board. Take your seats quietly, and remember all the shipboard safety rules that we went over in class."

"OK," Tamara, Belinda, Janet, Ellen, and Jessica chorused.

"Oh, wait just a second, you guys," Jessica said,

as the Unicorns started to hoist their totes and duffels. "Let me get a group shot. Maybe we can get Elizabeth to run it in the *Sixers*. You know, Unicorns on Board kind of thing."

"Good idea," Janet said. "Come on, let's line up. Ellen, Mandy, Tamara—you get in front and crouch down," she instructed them. "Where's Kimberly? Oh, there she is. Kimberly! Get over here!"

Kimberly Haver, who had been talking to Mr. Seigel, ran over. "I forgot to hand in my permission slip," she said breathlessly, assuming a model's pose next to Janet. "Mr. Seigel says they have to call my mom. But she just dropped me off, so obviously she thinks I can go. It's so dumb."

"Well, don't worry about that now. Here, Randy!" Jessica said, thrusting her camera in Randy's hand as he walked by. "Snap a couple of pictures of us, OK?"

"Um, OK," Randy said uncertainly, as Jessica struck a pose between Lila and Ellen.

The Unicorns all put on their best smiles, and Randy clicked a couple of pictures.

"Great!" Jessica said, taking the camera from Randy and tucking it back in her tote. "Those will be fabulous. I'll have copies made for everyone."

"Thanks, Jessica," Mandy said.

"Kimberly," Mr. Seigel called, "could you come here for a moment?"

Kimberly groaned. "I'll be right back, guys," she said. "You all go ahead and get on board. Save me a seat."

"OK," Jessica said, hoisting her tote bag. The wide tips of Elizabeth's fins stuck out of the top. Then she and the rest of the Unicorns headed down the wooden gangway to the boat.

"So did you bring it?" Jerry asked Bruce as they leaned against the boat railing.

"Sure did," Bruce gloated, patting his duffel. "Once we get to Santa Maria, we'll let the saps go off butterfly-hunting, and we'll just hang on the beach, surfing." He had to admit, it had been sheer genius to sneak his Boogie board along on the field trip. Sometimes he really outdid himself.

"Sounds like a plan to me," Jerry said, chortling.

Beneath their feet they felt the rumbling of large engines starting up. The sun was shining brightly, and the ocean was calm and a deep blue-green. Bruce lowered his Ray-Bans into position. "This is going to be cool," he said. "Extra science credit for hanging out on a beach all day with a bunch of babes."

"Yeah," Jerry agreed. "Too bad Mr. Seigel will be there. It'd be great if this was our own boat. Do you think your dad would ever let us take the cruiser out by ourselves?"

Bruce snorted. "Dream on, McAllister. That boat cost almost two hundred thousand dollars. Dad says I can't take it out till I'm sixteen. It takes three people just to run it, even with all the computer equipment." He kicked the white-painted metal railing of the *Island Dreamer*. "Not like this tub. I bet

I could run this thing all by myself. It probably has chipmunks down below, pedaling to keep the screws turning."

"Screws?" Jerry raised his eyebrows.

"Props," Bruce explained impatiently. "Propellers. I bet my dad's boat has three times the horsepower as this heap."

"Geez, really?" Jerry looked impressed.

"Sure," Bruce said. "This little boat is nothing. I bet I could run it with one hand tied behind my back."

"Actually, that might be difficult," a voice said in back of Bruce.

Frowning, Bruce turned to see some skinny nerd with red hair standing in back of him. Donald somebody, from school. "Yeah? Who says?"

Out of the corner of his eye, Bruce saw that Janet, Tamara, Aaron, Elizabeth, and Jessica had drifted over to hear the conversation.

"Well," the kid said, "it's just that a boat of this size does take at least two people to run it—partly because it's old-fashioned and probably not computerized. One person has to steer, and one person has to supervise the engines, run the radio, and plot the course on the sea charts."

"What makes you such an expert?" Bruce asked irritably. He could feel everyone's eyes on him.

"I'm not an expert," Donald said, shrugging his shoulders. "It's just a fact."

"It probably is harder to run an old-fashioned boat than a top-of-the-line modern one," Aaron mused.

"Yeah, but I don't think it would be easy for one seventh-grader to run anything much bigger than a Sunfish," Elizabeth said dryly, referring to the tiny sailboats the Sweet Valley Marina rented.

Bruce frowned at her. It was just like that goody-goody Wakefield to stick her nose into someone else's business. Well, he didn't have time to argue with her. "Come on, Jerry," Bruce said, slinging his duffel to his shoulder. "It's too crowded around here. Let's go snag some seats up front."

"Yeah," Jerry said, following Bruce toward the bow of the boat. "Let's ditch these geeks."

"Good old Bruce," Aaron said, leaning against the railing. "You always know what to expect from him: a lot of hot air."

Elizabeth grinned. "Too bad we're *not* on a sailboat—Bruce's bragging could keep our sails filled all day."

Maria and Amy laughed.

"Hey, what time is it, anyway?" Maria asked. "It seems like we've been here forever. Let's get this show on the road. Or this boat on the ocean, I mean."

Elizabeth checked her watch. "It's still only a couple minutes after eight." Shading her eyes, she saw her mom, Mr. Slater, and Mr. Seigel still on shore with a couple of other kids. The grown-ups seemed to be chatting with someone from the marina, and she could see Kimberly Haver waving her arms, arguing over something. "But we better get going soon."

"The engines are on," Amy said. "I can feel them. I can't wait to get out on the water. It's such a beautiful day."

"I hope we have time for a swim," Aaron said. "It's pretty hot already."

Just then the door to the pilothouse opened, and a man stuck his head out. "Hey, kid," he yelled to Aaron. "Cast us off, OK?"

"Sure," Aaron said. He moved to the bow of the boat and undid the thick rope there.

Amy, Elizabeth, and Maria all looked at one another excitedly.

"Won't be long now," Maria said, her dark eyes shining. She pulled a camera out of her small backpack. "You guys line up for a picture," she instructed, motioning them toward the side of the boat. "I want to document every minute of today."

Smiling, Amy and Elizabeth put their arms around each other and leaned against the rail. Maria snapped several pictures.

"Great," she said.

"Your finger wasn't over the lens, was it?" Elizabeth said, teasing her.

Maria pretended to look shocked. "Who, me? Are you implying that I'm not a total master when it comes to taking pictures?"

"I seem to remember you had a few problems with the video camera during those robberies at the Valley Mall," Elizabeth replied. "But maybe that's different."

"Oh, definitely," Maria said confidently. "But just in case, let's have Todd take some pictures of the three of us."

"Todd!" Elizabeth called him, and when he looked up, she waved him over. "Can you take a picture of us, please?"

"Sure." Todd took Maria's camera and carefully focused on the three girls. "Say 'extra credit,' everyone," he instructed, then he snapped the picture and returned the camera to Maria.

Aaron moved to the back of the boat and picked up the stern line. He unhooked it and threw the rope toward shore. Then he grinned at the girls and Todd and gave them a thumbs-up sign.

"The captain asked him to cast off," Elizabeth explained to Todd. "I guess we'll get going soon."

"Come on," Maria said, practically jumping up and down with anticipation. "Let's go grab our seats before the boat takes off."

In both the bow and the stern were wide benches that the boat's passengers usually sat on. The three girls had left their belongings on one, staking out their space.

As they headed down the side of the boat, the deck gave a little shudder beneath their feet. Elizabeth felt herself get excited all over again. It was a beautiful Saturday morning, and in just over an hour and a half, she was going to be exploring Santa Maria Island with her best friends.

"I can't believe it," Elizabeth said eagerly. "We'll

get to explore an island that's a remnant of an ancient volcanic eruption."

"And that's full of wildlife," Amy added. "Porpoises and starfish . . ."

"And jellyfish in the tidal pools," Elizabeth finished. She was glad she'd brought her own camera to take pictures of everything they saw.

The boat shuddered again, and Elizabeth instinctively grabbed the railing. She looked back at Maria, Todd, and Amy behind her.

"What was that?" Amy asked, her eyes surprised. She had grabbed the railing, too.

"This boat hasn't sprung a leak, has it?" Maria joked, holding on to Amy's shoulder.

Then Elizabeth glanced down toward the cement dock.

"We're moving!" she gasped, looking out to where Mr. Seigel, Mr. Slater, her mother, and a couple of classmates were still standing on shore. The dock was already a couple of feet away. "The boat is leaving!" she cried in alarm. "Mom!"

Three

◇

"Mom! Mr. Seigel!" Elizabeth yelled, leaning over the railing.

"Dad!" Maria screamed, cupping her hands around her mouth.

"Mr. Seigel!" Todd bellowed.

On shore, the three adults looked up in surprise. Mr. Seigel checked his watch, then started running down the dock toward the boat.

"Wait!" Elizabeth heard him yell. "Hold on!"

Mrs. Wakefield and Mr. Slater raced after the science teacher. They all looked alarmed as they ran to the end of the dock, waving at the boat.

"Come back!" Mr. Seigel shouted, but it was already hard to hear him over the noise of the engines. They were about thirty feet away from the marina, and the two huge propellers in back were churning up thick white channels of ocean.

Elizabeth, Todd, Maria, and Amy stared at one another.

"What's going on?" Todd asked in alarm. "The captain must have jumped the gun. Boy, I bet Mr. Seigel's pretty mad."

Maria nodded, her dark eyes flickering with anxiety. "I bet my dad is, too. I bet he's going to give the captain a talking-to."

"This has to be a mistake," Elizabeth said, fidgeting nervously with the end of her ponytail. "Or else it's just a warm-up, and he's going to circle the marina and then head back to the dock."

"Right, definitely," Maria agreed. "I'm sure that's what's going on."

"We'll head back to the dock in a minute," Amy said, a slight frown on her forehead. "No problem."

"No problem at all," Elizabeth repeated.

After all, they couldn't be headed out to sea with no grown-ups on board, could they?

"All right!" Jessica shouted, punching one fist in the air. "Santa Maria, here we come!"

She and the other Unicorns were sprawled on the wooden benches in the rear of the boat.

Lila yawned and stretched up toward the sun. "I guess Mr. Seigel's going to come over in a minute and start lecturing about all the stuff we're supposed to see today," she said. "Birds, sea mammals, plants, blah, blah, blah."

"Yeah. Too bad," Janet said, relaxing against an ice chest. She reached into her duffel and pulled out some suntan lotion.

Just then Jessica saw Elizabeth, Maria, Amy, Todd, and Aaron running down the aisle toward the back of the boat. Jessica noticed that Aaron, who was her sort-of boyfriend, looked very cute in cutoff jeans and a tank top that looked like a basketball jersey. She tossed her hair back and sat up straighter.

"Jessica!" Elizabeth cried, sliding onto the bench next to her sister. "We left Mom behind! And Mr. Seigel!"

"And my dad!" Maria added.

Jessica frowned. "What are you talking about?"

"Some guy asked me to cast off," Aaron explained hurriedly. "So I did. But I didn't think he was just going to take off like that!"

"What are you guys saying?" Janet demanded.

"Look around you," Maria said. "*We're* on the boat, heading toward the island. All the grown-ups are back on shore."

"So are a couple of other kids," Aaron said. "Like Peter Jeffries, and Brooke Dennis, and Kimberly Haver."

"You're kidding!" Jessica exclaimed, getting up and running to the side of the *Island Dreamer*. Sure enough, there, looking like very small, very upset dolls, were her mother, Mr. Seigel, and Mr. Slater, back on the dock. Mrs. Wakefield was cupping her hands around her mouth, shouting something, and Mr. Slater was waving his arms excitedly. Jessica could see Kimberly stomping around angrily, watching the departing boat.

"I don't believe this!" Jessica yelled, turning to the other Unicorns in delight. "We're free!"

"All right!" Janet said happily, waving to the adults on shore. They were hardly visible anymore.

"Free?"

Jessica looked up to see Elizabeth's blue-green eyes staring at her in disbelief.

"Free?" Elizabeth repeated. "Jessica, we're in a lot of trouble! We're not supposed to be on this boat without them. It could be dangerous!"

Jessica rolled her eyes. "Oh, Elizabeth, get a grip. What's so bad about it? The captain knows we're going to Santa Maria Island. So he'll take us there. We'll spend a fabulous day on the beach, have lunch, and come back home. No problems, no worries. And the best part is, it isn't even our fault. We won't get in any trouble for it." She and Lila slapped high fives, and Tamara and Janet started doing a little jig.

"Jessica's right, unbelievably enough," Bruce said, swaggering up to where they were standing. "This couldn't have worked out better if I'd planned it. Now we can just have a good time all day, without chasing a bunch of otters around." He paused, frowning. "I hope we still get the extra science credit, though. My grade totally needs it."

"You guys are crazy," Amy said, crossing her arms over her chest. "How can you be happy about this? Our parents are going to freak out. And Mr. Seigel could get in a lot of trouble. Everyone will blame him."

"Yeah," Elizabeth said. "This could mean that we won't ever do a fun field trip again."

"I don't know about you guys," Maria said, brushing her thick brown hair over her shoulders, "but I'm going to the captain right now and asking him to turn the boat around."

"That's a good idea," Elizabeth agreed. "I'll come with you."

"Me too," said Todd, already heading up toward the pilothouse.

"You guys are a bunch of wimps," Bruce taunted them. "You just don't know how to have fun."

"They're going to ruin everything," Janet complained. "Jessica, she's *your* twin. Stop her."

"Elizabeth!" Jessica said, running after her. "Wait up."

Elizabeth turned and faced her twin. "Jessica, there's no point in arguing. We need to turn this boat around."

Jessica looked at her sister pleadingly. "Why don't we just think about it for a minute, OK, Lizzie?" she wheedled. "I mean, what's the worst thing that can happen? You know this isn't our fault. Mom won't be mad at *us*. Why don't you just pretend that you didn't notice the grown-ups back on shore, and come sit down and relax? We could have a really good time today." Honestly, sometimes Elizabeth could be such a stick-in-the-mud. It was almost embarrassing, in front of the Unicorns.

"It just isn't right, Jessica," Elizabeth insisted. "We might as well turn around now, before we've gone too far."

Without waiting for an answer, Elizabeth headed back down the aisle to the pilothouse. Jessica watched her, a glum expression on her face. Then she went back and collapsed on a bench by Janet.

"Well?" Janet asked, shading her eyes against the sun.

"You know Elizabeth," Jessica said in resignation. "Once she makes up her mind about something, she's unstoppable. Oh, well. It was a fun idea, anyway."

The pilothouse was in the front of the boat, and it was taller than the large room where passengers sat if it was rainy. There was a short wooden door with a small window, and several other windows all around.

"Look," Elizabeth said in a low voice to Maria and Todd. "They have little curtains over all their windows. How do they see where they're going?"

Todd leaned forward and tried to look over the bow of the boat. "There's a window in front that's clear," he informed them. "But I can't see in."

Maria stepped up to the wooden door and

knocked briskly. "Hello?" she called loudly. "Excuse me? I need to speak to the captain, please, right away."

"What?" a voice came from inside.

"I said, I need to speak to the captain," Maria repeated more loudly.

"Um, what is it?" said a second voice.

Maria raised her eyebrows at Elizabeth. "He can't open the door?" she asked under her breath.

"We have a major problem out here," Elizabeth said loudly, putting her face right up toward the door. "We left the dock too early. All the grown-ups, all our chaperons, are still on shore. We have to turn back right away!" She wrung her hands. The longer they headed out to sea, the farther they were from shore, and the adults. If it took them too long to go back and pick up the rest of their group, they might have to cancel.

"Don't worry, kids," a muffled voice called back. "We'll be at the island in about an hour. Just sit down and be quiet."

Todd blinked in surprise. "What's wrong with him?" he asked softly. "Doesn't he even care that something's wrong?"

The boat continued to chug steadily out into the ocean, and there was no sign of its turning around. Elizabeth started to get angry.

"This is really bad," she said to Maria and Todd. "We shouldn't be out here by ourselves. How can we make him turn around?"

"Listen, kids," the voice called from inside the

pilothouse. "Everything's cool. We radioed your, uh, parents and told them to meet us at the island. They're not worried. They'll just take another boat there. OK? Now, just relax."

Elizabeth stared at Maria and Todd as Amy, Jessica, Janet, and Bruce joined them.

"What's going on?" Amy asked.

"They won't turn the boat around," Elizabeth said in disbelief. "The captain says not to worry."

"He says our parents and Mr. Seigel are taking another boat and meeting us at the island," Todd explained, scratching his head. "I guess that's OK."

"It just seems a little weird, that's all," Elizabeth said, still feeling concerned. "You'd think he would have checked to make sure everyone was on board before he took off."

"Maybe he's new to the charter business," Maria suggested. "Maybe he's not really sure of all the procedures or something."

"Yeah, maybe," Elizabeth said slowly.

Jessica was beaming. "So are you happy now? There's nothing to worry about. Let's just enjoy the boat ride."

Elizabeth hung back, her brow furrowed. "I don't know. It just seems—strange that the captain won't turn around, or even come out to talk to us."

"It seems like he should be more concerned," Amy added.

Jessica shrugged. "He's busy—he's got a boat to

run. You guys are just looking for something to worry about."

"Yeah. This kind of thing probably happens all the time," Bruce broke in. "He probably just doesn't want to waste fuel by going back. Why don't you leave him alone, now that you guys have ruined what was going to be a great day?"

"Yeah, Elizabeth," Janet said. "Just relax and quit trying to run everything for once."

"I don't always try to run everything!" Elizabeth protested, feeling stung by Janet's remark. She didn't usually try to run everything, did she? Then she cleared her throat. The situation still seemed kind of worrisome, but she knew she'd get nowhere trying to prove it to the Unicorns. Besides, they'd probably done all they could. "Maybe you're right," she said. "We might as well relax and try to enjoy the ride to the island."

"Way to go, Elizabeth," Jessica said. "See? You don't *have* to be a worrywart. Come on and sit by me. You can try this new mango-kiwi soda that Janet brought. It's fab."

With a sigh, Elizabeth followed her sister to the stern deck. There was a big difference between being a worrywart and being responsible, but she wasn't going to bother explaining that to Jessica.

"Par-ty!" Bruce stood on a bench and pretended to body-surf with the Boogie board he had sneaked onto the boat. His arms out at his sides, his toes hanging over the edge of the bench, he swayed back and forth, brushing imaginary waves off his face.

"Hey! Pass the chips!" Ellen Riteman said, sitting up on the towel that she had spread out on the wooden deck. Her sunglasses were pushed up on her nose, and she was holding a diet soda.

Laughing, Tamara tossed her the bag of chips. "This is almost as fun as a Unicorn meeting," she said, popping the top on her soda.

Jessica stretched out on her own towel. The sun was shining down, and she pulled her T-shirt over her head. "What a great day," she said happily, adjusting the straps of her purple bikini. She smiled at Elizabeth, who was sitting by the guardrail. Elizabeth smiled back.

Next to Jessica, Lila was putting her new Melody Power tape into the portable player. The first song, "Why Don't You Make Me Happy?" burst out at top volume.

"Excellent!" Lila yelled, standing up and starting to dance.

Within seconds, Janet, Ellen, Tamara, and Ken Matthews were all dancing to the beat. Aaron, Winston, and Todd pushed some of the benches out of the way to give them more room.

On her towel, Jessica tapped her feet to the rhythm. The field trip was just getting better and better. Too bad they would be arriving at the island so soon—it was cool to just be gliding over the waves on their very own private boat. It wouldn't be the same once they got to the island and the grown-ups arrived.

"Jessica, get up," Lila said, tapping her lightly with a bare foot. "I want to show you this new move I learned."

Elizabeth pulled her feet under her bench out of the way as Jessica, Lila, Janet, and Ellen all lined up and began to practice the latest dance step.

"Yeah, that's it," Lila said, pivoting to the left. "Now cross your feet, and . . ."

"I got it, I got it," Jessica said, laughing, clapping her hands to the music, her long blond hair swinging in the wind. "And once to the right, and turn . . ."

Elizabeth had to admit that all that dancing looked like fun, but somehow she couldn't get into the partying spirit. Instead, she wandered over to the end of the stern, where Randy Mason was pointing some of his instruments in the general direction of the shore.

I might as well try to collect stuff for my article, she thought, pulling out her notebook. "What are you working on, Randy?"

Randy frowned. "I thought I was experimenting with a sonar-based course-tracking system," he explained. "But something's wrong. It doesn't seem to be gauging our distance or direction properly."

"Is it an instrument malfunction?" Elizabeth asked, writing down his comments.

"I don't know." Randy shook his head. "It

worked fine yesterday, when I tested it. But now the readings are all screwed up. Or maybe I'm just doing something wrong."

"Oh. Well, let me know if you get it working," Elizabeth told him. She closed her notebook and sat back down on a bench. It was almost a quarter to ten. They should be at the island any minute now. Shading her eyes, she gazed out over the ocean, waiting to see the dim blue outline of the island pop into view. Maybe if she looked really closely, she'd be able to see the boat carrying her mom and Mr. Seigel and Mr. Slater, heading for the island, too. But all she saw was water.

Four

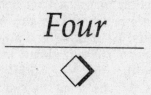

"This is getting kind of lame," Bruce said, staring out at the ocean. "I mean, how long is it supposed to take to get to the island?"

"It was supposed to take only about an hour and a half," Todd said, coming to stand next to him. "But we're running late."

Bruce nodded. Wilkins was on the basketball team with him, and he was a decent player, but other than that Bruce didn't have much use for him. He was always hanging around old goody-goody Elizabeth Wakefield.

"Maybe we're going slower than they usually do," Jerry commented, leaning over the guardrail and letting the wake splash his fingers.

"Whatever," Bruce muttered. "All I know is, I'm tired of this boat—I'm ready to hit the beach."

Jerry and Todd both nodded their agreement.

Bruce glanced at the group of girls a few feet away. They were still dancing and hanging out.

"Did anyone see that movie *Island Paradise* last night on TV?" Cammi Adams asked. She was a sixth-grader, and she looked it, Bruce thought dryly. Straight up and down.

Cammi rubbed more sunscreen onto her fair skin.

"No," Amy said, wiping the sweat off her forehead with her T-shirt. "What was it about?"

Inwardly, Bruce groaned. Why couldn't girls talk about something interesting, like the game that had been on cable last night? Next thing he knew, they'd probably start going on and on about shoes or something. He hung over the side of the boat and watched the waves splash against the hull.

"I saw it," Grace Oliver joined in. "It was really neat. This boat full of people got shipwrecked on an island, and everyone fell in love with everyone else."

Bruce groaned out loud this time.

"It was really romantic," Janet agreed, not paying attention to him. She looked around the deck, frowning thoughtfully. "You know, that boat was a lot like this one."

"Maybe we'll get shipwrecked," Tamara said dreamily. "We'll be stuck forever on some beautiful island, and we'll all wear grass skirts and flowers in our hair."

That did it. Leaning over, Bruce spat loudly into the water. These girls were nutcases. "There is *no* way you're getting me into a grass skirt," he said threateningly.

Everyone laughed, and feeling pleased with himself, Bruce flicked some hair off his forehead.

"Not that you don't have the legs for it," Todd commented.

Bruce decided to ignore that remark. "Actually, I read a book once about a bunch of kids who got shipwrecked on a desert island," he told the girls with a grin.

"You actually read a book? That's news," Belinda said, looking at her fingernails.

Bruce glared at her.

"What happened?" Jerry asked.

Bruce pried his eyes from Belinda. "It was a bunch of boys from a boarding school," he explained, thinking back to the story he'd read. "An English boarding school. And they ended up on an island with no grown-ups." He paused to get people's reactions.

"Like us," Ken added.

"Uh-huh."

"So what happened?" Jerry repeated.

"They all ended up killing each other," Bruce said smugly. "Like cannibals. In fact, they roasted this one—"

"Oh, Bruce," Janet groaned, tossing her suntan lotion at him.

"It's true," he insisted. "It was right there in the book."

* * *

"No, Jessica," Lila said. "You have to bounce on the *second* beat. Like this." She demonstrated the dance step again.

"You messed up, too," Jessica said critically, counting the beats of "Beat Boogie Baby." She took off her baseball cap and wiped her forehead. It was only a little past ten, but it was really hot. She couldn't wait to get to the island and splash around in the surf.

Lila knit her eyebrows. "Yeah, I guess I did. Is there something wrong with the music? The rhythm's all weird." Closing her eyes, she listened for a minute, snapping her fingers in time to the heavy bass sounds.

"Yeah," she said, opening her eyes. "There *is* something wrong with the music." Leaning over, she snapped off the tape player.

"Hey, what's the big idea?" Bruce demanded. "Let's have some tunes."

"Turn it back on, Lila," Janet commanded, brushing back her hair. "We were just getting going."

"Wait a second," Lila said, holding up her hand. "Listen to that."

Jessica couldn't hear anything but the noisy splashing of the large propellers in back of them, leaving a wide, white wake. The hum of the engines vibrated beneath her feet, and the wind whistled in her ears.

"There it is," Lila cried. "Listen."

Jessica stood still, straining to hear. Finally she thought she heard what Lila meant. She could feel a heavier vibration, almost a pounding, coming from somewhere on the boat.

"Where's that coming from? Is that the engine?" Jessica asked.

"Where's *what* coming from?" Bruce asked. "You girls are hearing things."

"No, it's there," Lila insisted. "Someone's banging on something. How totally annoying. It's completely wrecking my concentration."

"Really," Jessica said. "How are we supposed to follow the music with that irritating banging sound?"

"I wonder if something's wrong with the propellers," Mandy said, looking concerned.

"Where's it coming from?" Aaron asked.

"I don't know," Jessica said, "but I'm going to find out. Whoever's making that noise has to stop right now. We're trying to listen to the new Melody Power tape!"

When Jessica and Lila went into the main room on the charter boat, Jessica saw it wasn't very big: just a white-painted square lined with more benches. There were a few windows to let in light, and a couple of doors marked "Buoys" and "Gulls."

"So where's that noise coming from?" Lila demanded. She stalked over to the door marked "Gulls" and flung it open. The rest room was empty.

"I'm not checking 'Buoys,'" Jessica said. "But I

don't think the sound is coming from there." The noise definitely seemed louder inside the passenger room, Jessica decided. She started walking around, trying to see where the noise was the loudest.

"Then where?" Lila said. "Is the captain hammering something? This noise is driving me crazy!"

"Li, come over here," Jessica said. She was leaning next to a door marked "Supplies." It really sounded like the pounding noise was coming from there. "Maybe something has come loose and is whacking against something else," Jessica suggested.

Lila nodded. "Let's fix it. It's starting to give me à headache." She reached out and jiggled the metal door handle, but it seemed to be stuck.

"Hang on." Jessica took off her sneaker and smacked it against the handle as hard as she could. Then she squeezed the little catch, and with a tiny click, the door swung outward.

"Whoa, total darkness," Jessica murmured. She leaned in the door and waited for her eyes to adjust to the dim light.

When they did, she let out a sharp, horrified gasp.

"Where's Jessica?" Elizabeth asked, squinting in the bright sun. She was sitting on one of the ice chests, she and Todd were sharing a soda, and she was really starting to relax. She had to admit, even with the little hitch about the grown-ups not being on board, it was turning into a great day. The sun was shining, the water was blue, she was with all her best friends . . . and in just a few minutes they would be at a beautiful wildlife sanctuary.

Janet pointed toward the passenger room. "She and Lila went to investigate that weird noise."

"They're not back yet?" Elizabeth checked her watch. "Hey, you know, it's almost ten thirty. I thought it took only an hour and a half to get to the island. Shouldn't we have gotten there by now?"

"Yeah, you'd think so," Winston said, staring out at the ocean. "It's funny, but I don't even see any land—anywhere."

Elizabeth stood up. "Me neither, and I've been looking. But I'm sure we'll be there soon—maybe the sun is making a haze on the water so we can't see land until we're right on top of it. In the meantime, I'm going to go find Jessica."

"I'll come with you," Winston said, putting down the book he was trying to read.

"We might as well all go," Amy said, standing up and stretching. "I haven't been inside yet anyway."

"The bathrooms are inside, aren't they?" Todd asked.

In the passenger room, it took Elizabeth a moment before she saw Lila and Jessica standing like statues in front of the open supply closet.

"Jessica?" she called. "What's going on?"

In reply, Jessica turned around and wordlessly pointed into the supply closet. She and Lila both looked scared, and they started to back away.

Elizabeth, Winston, Todd, and Amy all crowded around.

"What is it?" Elizabeth asked. "How come you guys opened the supply door?"

Leaning in the open door, her eyes searched the crowded shelves for whatever had spooked her sister. Then she saw the two huddled shapes on the floor.

"Good grief!" she whispered. Inside the store-room were two men, all tied up! One man was wearing a white captain's uniform, and the other was in navy blue work clothes. They were both unconscious, and the crewman's forehead had a thin trickle of blood on it.

Elizabeth felt her heart start to pound. What could this mean? Suddenly her uneasiness about the field trip rose up inside her again—only much more sharply than before. As Elizabeth and her friends stood there, frozen, the man in the white uniform opened his eyes groggily and blinked at them. "Did you hear me knocking?" he asked weakly.

"Yes," Jessica whispered, staring at him.

Elizabeth swallowed hard. "Who—who are you?" she asked, trying to sound brave. "What happened here?"

"I'm Captain Thomas Moreland," the man said, his words a little slurred. "I own the *Island Dreamer*. This is my crewman, Walt Lufkin. We've been hijacked. I've been pounding, trying to get someone's attention. . . ."

"Hijacked!" Maria cried, staring at him. "What do you mean?"

The captain weakly held up his hands, which had been lashed together with a length of rope. "We were waiting for our charter this morning when two guys came on board and knocked us out. I remember they had a cloth covered with something that smelled sweet—they made us breathe it."

"Some kind of drug," Winston whispered. "Like ether or something."

Elizabeth suddenly felt light-headed. It was much worse than she had imagined. The day had started with such promise, and now—and now who knew what would happen to them?

The captain squinted up at Elizabeth. "You must be the school field trip who chartered us. Where are we?"

"We don't know," Elizabeth said shakily. "We left the dock two and a half hours ago, but we haven't reached Santa Maria Island yet. So the guys running the boat are the guys who knocked you out?" Her throat felt as though it were closing in fear, and her mind was racing, trying to put the pieces together.

The captain nodded ruefully, then groaned and put his head back down on the floor. "Yeah," he muttered, his voice sounding weaker. "They must be."

"Does anyone have a knife or something?" Elizabeth asked urgently, turning to her friends. "We've got to cut them loose!"

Next to the captain, the crewman groaned and shifted his weight, but his eyes stayed shut.

"I've got one," Winston said, pulling out a Swiss Army knife. He knelt and began cutting the captain's hands loose. "But it doesn't look like it'll do much good," he added quietly.

After Captain Moreland's hands were finally freed, he opened his eyes again. But Elizabeth thought he looked even worse than before—his face was clammy and gray, and his eyes were unfocused.

"You've got to wake up," she said desperately, shaking his shoulder. "You've got to help us. If we've been hijacked, we're in serious trouble. And we don't have any other adults to help us."

"What about on the island?" Todd asked. "Will there be some wildlife specialists there?"

The captain shook his head with great effort, and his mouth tightened with pain. "These guys aren't headed for the island," he said softly.

"Oh, my gosh," Maria breathed. "Those guys must have been lying when they said they had called our parents on shore. I bet no one has any idea where we are!"

Elizabeth felt a fresh surge of panic. No one knew where they were—that thought hadn't even occurred to her. They were being hijacked. They were far out to sea with two ruthless boat thieves, and no one to help them except two men who weren't even able to sit up. She swallowed hard, trying desperately to keep her head.

At her feet the captain was groggily rubbing his hands where they had been tied. Winston had cut the crewman free, but he was still unconscious and didn't move.

"Why would those guys hijack this boat?" Elizabeth asked, kneeling in front of Captain Moreland. "It isn't very fast or powerful."

"That's just it," the captain said, leaning back and closing his eyes sleepily. "It's inconspicuous. And we were due to leave the marina anyway, on this charter. So I guess they figured no one would miss us until tonight, when we don't come home."

"You said we weren't heading for the island anymore. Do you have any idea where these guys are taking us?" Winston asked, folding his knife and putting it back in his pocket.

Captain Moreland took several shallow breaths before answering. "My guess is Mexico. I think they must have committed some crime, and they're fleeing U.S. waters."

"But Mexico isn't safe for them," Todd pointed out. "The government will just send them back."

The captain shrugged helplessly. "Maybe they're meeting someone there—someone who will hide them."

"OK," Maria said in a tense voice. "Say we're going to Mexico. How long will it take us to get there?"

"About ten hours," the captain said, rubbing his hand across his eyes. "But we're not going to make it."

"Why not?" Todd asked, his voice sounding thin and scared.

"There's a big storm coming in from the north," the captain explained wearily. "It was supposed to catch up with us by about five o'clock, but it seems to be moving faster than that. It's going to be really bad, and a boat this size won't be able to handle it."

Todd bit his lip. "When you say, 'won't be able to handle it—'"

"I mean it's going to blow us out of the water." Captain Moreland grimaced in pain and closed his eyes again. When he turned his head, Elizabeth could see the big, bruised lump on his temple where he must have been hit, just like Walt. She swallowed hard. This was a total disaster. If only Mr. Seigel, Mr. Slater, and her mother could have been on board! Elizabeth was sure that between the three of them, they could have handled things somehow.

Then Elizabeth took a deep breath. *Get a grip*, she commanded herself. The fact was, there *weren't* any adults around, and it was up to them—herself and her classmates—to get them out of this mess. Elizabeth couldn't afford to lose her cool.

Kneeling on the floor, Elizabeth gently touched the captain's shoulder, trying to keep him awake. "What can we do?" she asked urgently. "How can we stop them?"

For long moments, the captain lay silently on the storeroom floor. His eyes were closed, and his face was gray. Elizabeth met Todd's eyes, then Jessica's. Everyone looked as scared as she felt. Still unconscious, the crewman groaned. Elizabeth felt a shiver of fear snake down her back.

"They control the shortwave radio," the captain finally mumbled. "In the pilothouse. But there's a small CB radio in my private quarters. Call for help. Say mayday, SOS . . ." His voice weakened and trailed off, and his head lolled to one side. He had passed out again.

"I don't think there's much we can do for them," Elizabeth said quietly, standing up. "Maybe they need to sleep off whatever drug the hijackers used. Let's just try to make them comfortable."

Winston and Todd nodded stiffly, then pulled and pushed Captain Moreland and Walt Lufkin into more comfortable positions on the floor. Elizabeth stood to the side, trying to remember some first-aid techniques they had learned in health class. *Come on,* she urged herself. *There must be something you can do.* But her brain was having trouble processing things right now.

Everyone else is doing something, and you're just standing around. She watched as Maria and Amy carried several rough, musty blankets from the storeroom shelves and draped them over the injured seamen. Jessica tentatively pushed rolled-up blankets under their heads.

"Are they in shock?" Jessica asked worriedly. "Do we need to do CPR or something?"

"I don't know," Elizabeth said helplessly. "They're both still breathing. All we can do is keep them warm."

"I remember something about keeping their feet elevated," Amy said, looking down at the men in concern.

"Maybe these will work." Todd reached for some large packages of paper towels and propped the men's feet up on them. Then they all backed quietly out of the storeroom and closed the door behind them.

Elizabeth felt shaky and more fearful than she ever had in her life.

"This really bites," Lila said bitterly, putting one hand on her hip. "Some great field trip."

"No duh, Lila. Tell us something we don't know," Jessica said irritably. She turned to Elizabeth. "What now?"

Elizabeth frowned in concentration. *They're counting on you*, she thought. *You're the levelheaded one who always has great ideas, remember? You have to think of something.* "The first thing we have to do—" Elizabeth broke off and swallowed hard. It wasn't any use. She didn't have a solitary clue what they should do. Her brain had frozen.

Five

"What we need is a plan," Todd said, pacing back and forth, his face worried.

Elizabeth nodded and motioned Jessica, Maria, Amy, Lila, and Winston closer. They huddled together in the middle of the large passenger room. She was glad to be surrounded by her best friends—it even helped to have Lila around.

"Todd's right," Jessica murmured, looking over her shoulder. "But where do we start?"

"Dad says the first thing to do is evaluate your position," Lila said, nodding firmly. "Then you find your enemy's weakness and go in for the kill."

Elizabeth grinned despite herself. Before she had a chance to comment on Lila's sudden fighting spirit, Janet Howell walked in.

"Did someone say something about an enemy?"

she asked. "Where have you all been? What's going on?" She paused in front of a mirror fastened to the wall between the "Buoys" room and the "Gulls." "Wow, my nose is getting pink," she murmured. "I better put some more lotion on it."

As she rummaged through her bag, Bruce walked into the large room. "Hey, is this where the bathrooms are?" he asked loudly. "Oh, there they are." He headed for the one marked "Buoys."

Soon the passenger room was filled with almost everyone who had been out on the deck just minutes before. The smell of coconut suntan lotion filled the air. When everyone was gathered together, Elizabeth quickly filled them in. Seeing her classmates' eyes go wide, their mouths drop open, made her more determined to keep herself together. Maybe later, when she was safe at home, she would panic and fall apart. But right now she just didn't have time.

"So now we're coming up with a plan," she finished, keeping one eye on the door. She didn't want the hijackers to walk in on their planning session.

Bruce narrowed his eyes strategically. "I'd hate to subject anyone to my karate moves, but it looks like I might have to. Desperate times call for desperate—"

"I don't think karate will be necessary, Bruce," Elizabeth said patiently. *Geez, what a fathead.* "We're all going to have to work together if we're going to get out of this."

"Yeah," Ken said. He glanced at Bruce. "Good

thing you could sail this tub with one hand behind your back. That might come in handy."

"Huh? Oh, yeah. Right." Bruce shuffled his feet uncomfortably.

"There *is* one bright side to all this," Randy Mason said thoughtfully.

Maria raised her eyebrows. "There is?"

A smile spread across Randy's face. "It means all my instruments aren't wrong after all. It was the *boat* that was headed in the wrong direction." He chuckled. "What a relief. I thought I had done all that work for nothing."

Elizabeth sighed. That wasn't any great consolation to her, but if it made him feel better, who was she to argue?

"Well, I don't see how your instruments are going to get us out of this," Jessica said. "What we need is someone who will really take charge. A natural leader. Someone we can count on in a crisis. Someone like Janet Howell."

Janet smiled radiantly and adjusted the strap of her bikini. "Well, I don't like to brag, but I *am* a natural leader. I have a lot of experience as the president of the Unicorns and the head Booster. As you know."

"As we all know," Jessica agreed. "So what kind of ideas do you have?"

"Ideas?" Janet frowned.

Amy sighed impatiently. "Listen, you guys, being hijacked at sea isn't exactly the same as running a Unicorn meeting."

"Yeah," Maria said wryly. "For one thing, it doesn't matter what we're wearing."

"Oh, ha ha," Janet said, her eyes narrowing. "Let me tell you—"

"Look, we have to quit arguing," Elizabeth broke in. "We're all in . . . the same boat, so to speak. We need to cooperate. Now, I propose that we split into groups. One small group will find the captain's private quarters and look for the CB. Everyone else will go back on deck and try to look normal. Play music, dance, have snacks, whatever. So far the hijackers have stayed in the pilothouse, but if they venture out, we want them to think that we don't know anything is wrong."

"That's a good plan," Todd said, patting Elizabeth on the shoulder.

"I'll look for the radio," Winston volunteered bravely.

Elizabeth looked at him gratefully. "I will, too," she said.

"Count me in," said Maria. "I'll feel better if I'm with you," she told Elizabeth, who smiled at her.

"Me too," Amy said. "My uncle has a CB in his truck. Maybe I'll remember how to use it."

"I volunteer to go back on deck and look normal," Bruce said casually, brushing his hair back.

Todd groaned. "Figures," he muttered.

"Shut up, Wilkins," Bruce said.

"Stop it, both of you," Lila said with a frown. She motioned everyone toward the door. "Come on, you guys. Let's go back on deck and play music. We could even eat some lunch or something. Remember, we have to look as if we don't know anything's wrong."

"I just hope we can do it," Tamara said under her breath.

"I guess we look pretty normal," Jessica said in a low voice to Lila. "That is, normal if we were at someone's funeral."

Everyone except Elizabeth, Winston, Maria, and Amy was gathered on the stern deck, where the sun was still shining brightly. But all the fun had gone out of the day. Instead of running around, dancing and laughing, and playing loud music, everyone on the field trip was stiffly lined up on benches, looking miserable. Jessica had seen more excitement at a social studies exam.

"Turn on the tape player, Lila," Janet said. "We could listen to Johnny Buck."

Lila switched tapes and flicked the player on.

"We're pausing in our regular programming to bring you this late-breaking news flash," the radio announcer said, as Lila stood up and started walking toward the center of the deck.

"Oops, wrong button," Lila said, turning back.

"Early this morning the First National Bank of Sweet Valley was robbed by two men who made off with almost five million dollars' worth of cash and bearer bonds," the announcer continued.

"Oh, my gosh," Mandy breathed. "Turn that up, Lila."

After quickly looking to make sure the hijackers were nowhere in sight, Lila cranked up the volume. Jessica perched on the edge of her bench, straining to hear the news report over the noise of the churning waves.

"The two men were described by onlookers as being white, in their mid-thirties. One has sandy hair, the other one dark brown. They were described as looking rough and unkempt and should be considered armed and dangerous."

"Oh, man," Tamara moaned.

"Shh!" Jessica hissed, waving her hands to silence her.

"Their present whereabouts are unknown, but authorities believe they may have escaped by stealing a boat from the Sweet Valley Marina," the announcer continued. "To repeat: Two bank thieves are on the loose, and are armed and dangerous. There is a one-hundred-thousand-dollar reward for information leading to their capture. Anyone knowing their location or destination should notify the authorities immediately. This station will keep you posted with up-to-the-minute reports as the situation develops. And now back to our regularly scheduled programming of danceable tunes and romantic hits."

Jessica felt her heart sink down to her sneakers. Today was really turning into a total bummer. Next to her, Lila snapped off the radio and sat there looking kind of pale green. Jessica glanced around and saw that pretty much everyone had a dying-cow face on.

Ellen raised her hand. "I know their whereabouts and location," she said weakly. "Does this mean I get a reward?"

Jessica forced herself to smile. "I guess we all get to split it," she told Ellen. Then she set her jaw determinedly. She'd always thought that she had what it took to be a real leader—even to be the next Unicorn president, after Janet went off to Sweet Valley High School next year. Now was her chance to show her leadership qualities. And maybe next time the club elections rolled around, her fellow Unicorns would remember. "OK, Lila, put on that Johnny Buck tape. And Tamara, hand me a Diet Coke and some chips. We have to look unsuspicious—like a bunch of kids who don't know anything."

In another minute the loud sounds of *Bucking the System* filled the air. Todd and Ken opened the ice chests and started passing sandwiches and cookies around, but most people weren't very hungry. Jessica lay back down on her towel and put on her sunglasses. *Jessica Wakefield, born leader.* She liked the sound of that. Too bad she was too scared about being hijacked at sea by two armed and dangerous men to appreciate it completely.

"OK, here's a little passageway," Elizabeth whispered, pushing open a door. At the opposite end of the passenger room, a small hall led to the minuscule galley on one side and the captain's room on the other. The galley was dark, with only one small porthole high above the stainless-steel counter. Elizabeth saw a microwave, cupboards, a two-ring hot plate, a coffee percolator, and two fold-down stools. Obviously, the boat was never intended to feed its passengers.

On the other side of the hall from the galley was the captain's quarters. It, too, was a small dark room with only one porthole looking out over the side of the boat. There was a narrow built-in bunk along one wall and a cluttered wooden desk under the window.

"I guess we should start looking in the cupboards and drawers," Winston said in a soft voice, closing the door behind him.

Maria snapped on the desk lamp. "Yeah," she agreed. "He sort of gave us permission to. And it's a matter of . . ."

"Life and death," Amy finished grimly.

Elizabeth was already opening some of the built-in storage cabinets. She felt kind of weird, going through a stranger's belongings, but Amy was right—it *was* a matter of life and death. "I'm not sure what a CB looks like," she confessed, "but I guess it'll seem pretty obvious when we find it."

Every minute that passed felt like an hour as they searched the room thoroughly. Elizabeth could feel beads of sweat on her forehead, and her hands were clammy. The rumbling of the engines made the floor vibrate beneath her feet, and every little sound made her startle and jump. She felt as though her nerves were stretched to their breaking point. *If only I had woken up sick this morning,* she thought ruefully. Then she shrugged off the idea. *What's with you, Elizabeth Wakefield? Since when are you such a total wimp?*

"Wait! I found it!" Winston cried, pulling a bundle of cords and headphones from a drawer.

"Quick, let's set it up," Maria said, crowding closer to him.

He plugged in the headphones and rapidly flipped knobs and dials. The lights on the square box started to glow amber and green.

"We have to find the right channel," Amy said. "Slow down and start to listen for other people talking."

Elizabeth crossed the fingers on both hands and watched as Winston slowly turned the knobs one notch at a time.

All of a sudden his eyes lit up and he bounced on his heels. "I've got something!" Carefully he turned the knob until the channel came through clearly, then he pressed the talk button.

"Mayday, mayday!" he cried. "Someone please help us!"

"Who's there?" a startled voice came back.

"This is Winston Egbert," Winston said into the handset. "I'm on a charter boat, and we've been hijacked."

"Hijacked! Is this a joke?"

"No, it's not a joke!" Maria cried into the handset. "Please help us!"

"Our boat is the *Island Dreamer*," Winston said. "We were hijacked out of the Sweet Valley Marina. Please call the coast guard!"

Sitting in the desk chair, Elizabeth felt as if her heart were beating in her throat. This had to work, she thought desperately. These people had to save them—or else all their lives might be in danger. There was no telling when Captain Moreland or Walt Lufkin would recover—it could be hours from now. Hours they didn't have.

"Where are you?" the voice asked.

"We don't know," Winston responded unhappily. "We were supposed to be heading to Santa Maria Island, but I don't know where we're going now. Maybe Mexico."

"You don't know where you're heading for sure?" the voice asked.

"No," Winston insisted. "We're just a bunch of kids on a field trip—but our parents got left on shore. And the boat has been hijacked by two—"

At that moment the captain's door crashed open. Elizabeth gasped and shrank back in her chair. A tall, burly man with sandy-blond hair stood there, looking fierce.

"You were right," he said over his shoulder to someone. "You did hear something. A bunch of pesky kids." He leaned over and effortlessly ripped the CB out of Winston's hand.

"Hello? Hello? Are you there?" a voice was saying. But the hijacker yanked the handset out of the box.

Elizabeth's heart shriveled to the size of a pebble. Winston met her eyes. His face was ashen. Obviously, he understood the situation as well as she did: There went their last chance of rescue!

Six

◇

The sandy-haired man leaned back against the door, his arms crossed over his chest, the ruined CB dangling from one hand. "So we have a bunch of kids who seem to know what's going on," he said in a mean voice. "What should we do with them?"

Another man laughed behind him, and the sound made Elizabeth grit her teeth. Maria and Amy were both still sitting on the floor. Maria was gripping the edge of Amy's shirt. Amy's face looked frozen with fear.

Sandy Hair stood back and jerked his head toward the open doorway. "Come on, kids," he said. "Back on deck where we can keep an eye on you."

Elizabeth glanced at Winston and Maria and Amy. She was paralyzed by confusion and fear. A million thoughts were running through her head, fast and jumbled-up. Did the hijackers know they had found the captain and the crewman? What were they going to do now? Should the kids cooperate? And if both hijackers were here, who was steering the boat?

Sandy Hair's eyes narrowed when the four friends didn't budge. He cuffed Winston roughly on the shoulder, making him fall over. "Move!" the man yelled loudly, pointing out the door.

That did it. Elizabeth, Maria, and Amy all scrambled to their feet, and Elizabeth grabbed Winston's arm and pulled him after her. Out in the hall, a slightly smaller man with dark, unkempt hair pushed them roughly up the passageway and into the passenger room. Almost staggering, Elizabeth held on to Winston as they headed back onto the deck. Their eyes met, and an unspoken thought passed between them: What was going to happen to them now?

"I hope Elizabeth and the others have found that radio by now," Lila said, crouching next to where Jessica was lying on her towel. She pushed her sunglasses up on her nose.

"Yeah," Jessica said, shading her eyes to look up at Lila. "I just can't believe this is happening to us. I wish I had gone to the mall today instead."

Lila nodded. "Or we could have all hung out at my house," she said. "I mean, you could get just as good a tan by my pool as you could on some stupid boat." She sighed dramatically. "But nooo," she continued. "I had to try and pull my science grade up. And what do I get for that? Hijacked!"

"It seems so unfair," Jessica said wearily. "I mean, it's like a message that we shouldn't try to get extra credit or something." She knew that extra credit wasn't exactly the reason the Unicorns had decided to go on the field trip, but she decided not to mention that fact.

"We have to take our minds off of what's happening," Janet said, opening a bag of cookies and taking a few out. "I move that we start making plans for the next Unicorn extravaganza."

Jessica sat up, feeling a twinge of interest. "Good idea," she said immediately. "We haven't done anything major in a long time. What should we do? A huge Unicorn party? Maybe we should organize a Unicorn-appreciation week at school."

A few feet away, Bruce snorted, but Jessica ignored him. For the past ten minutes, he and Jerry had been practicing karate moves on each other. Jessica thought they looked pretty silly.

"Maybe a party," Janet said thoughtfully. "But a party with a theme. After all, there has to be some excuse to let non-Unicorns come."

"Maybe we could try to raise money for something," Belinda suggested, blowing a bubble with her gum. "Like for new Booster uniforms."

"Yeah," Jessica said excitedly. "After all, we already have cute uniforms for the fall and winter—but what about little summer uniforms? I saw some really adorable ones in a TV movie. Did anyone see *Cheerleader for a Day* a couple of months ago?"

"Uh-uh," Lila said, taking out her suntan oil. "They wore cute uniforms in it?"

"Uh-huh," Jessica confirmed. "They had all these great sequins on them. That's what we need. Our Booster uniforms are fine, but we need to go big-time with them."

"That's a good idea, Jessica," Janet said approvingly. "So let's have a big party and raise money for new Booster uniforms. We can charge people like two dollars to get in, and we can have all sorts of great food, and maybe a live band—"

"Hey, cut it out!" Winston's angry voice interrupted Janet.

Startled, Jessica looked toward the passenger room.

Rough hands shoved Winston out the door, then Elizabeth, then Maria and Amy. They each hit the guardrail with a little "oof," then caught themselves against the side.

Jessica leaped to her feet and ran to Elizabeth. "Are you OK?" she asked urgently.

A huge man grabbed her by the shoulders and shoved her back. "Stay away from her, kid." He peered first at Elizabeth, then at Jessica, then at Elizabeth again. "Hey, Jack," he said to the dark-haired man. "Lookit what we have here. Twins."

"Aw, ain't that sweet, Gary?" Jack replied. He came out of the passenger room holding a large coil of thin rope.

These must be the two hijackers, Jessica thought, staying close to Elizabeth. *Talk about creepy-looking guys.*

Behind Jessica, Lila turned off the music, and everyone gathered around hesitantly. The only sound was the churning of the waves behind them as they headed out to sea.

"OK, kids," Gary said loudly, brushing his dirty-blond hair back. "Looks like you know this field trip is taking a little detour. I want everyone to line up here, against the rail." With one thick, stumpy finger he gestured to the rail, where Elizabeth was huddled with Winston, Maria, and Amy.

Gary walked behind the row of kids, poking each one in turn.

"Hey, cut that out!" Bruce demanded when Gary poked him in the ribs.

Gary stopped cold. "*What* did you say to me?"

"I said—"

"Bruce!" Jessica hissed, shooting him a warning look.

But Bruce wasn't listening to her. He and Jerry were exchanging looks, and in the next instant, they'd both turned around, their fists clenched.

Oh, please, Jessica thought fearfully, hoping Bruce would pick up her brain waves. *Please don't practice your tough act now.*

But Bruce didn't seem to get the message. "Hai-yah!" he and Jerry chorused as they flung their legs through the air in a karate kick. At least, Jessica thought, it was probably supposed to be a karate kick.

Gary gave a snort of derision and stepped quickly sideways, and Bruce and Jerry both sailed past him. Then they landed in two heaps, on the deck.

"Ow!" Bruce said, rubbing his skinned knee.

Jerry grunted in pain as he slid across the deck right into a bench.

Jessica cringed. It had been kind of birdbrained for Bruce and Jerry to try that stupid kick, but she hated to see them get hurt.

"Look, kids," Gary said impatiently, "quit doing stupid stuff—you're just going to get hurt. Now, everyone line up against the rail, like we told you. Come on, move!"

Gary nudged Bruce in the ribs with his booted foot. Limping, his knee bloody, Bruce got to his feet and stood next to the rail. Jessica edged closer to Elizabeth, and slowly, one by one, the other field-trippers got into line against the rail.

"Hey, what are you doing?" Jerry cried as Jack, the dark-haired hijacker, lashed his hands to the railing with his rope.

Jack laughed wickedly. "What does it look like I'm doing, dimwit?"

Cringing, Jessica turned away as Jack moved down the line of kids, tying everyone's hands to the railing. "Did you find the radio?" she whispered to Elizabeth.

Elizabeth nodded. "We put out a mayday call, but we got interrupted," she whispered back. "I don't know if it did any good or not. We couldn't tell them where we were."

Jessica bit her lip as she imagined spending the rest of her life on a boat in the middle of nowhere with a couple of evil hijackers. A couple of evil hijackers who were getting awfully close to tying her hands to the railing.

"Ouch," Belinda Layton said, a couple feet up from them. "That's too tight."

"Shut up," Jack snarled. Belinda's eyes teared up, and she looked out at the water.

Then Jack came to tie Elizabeth, who winced as the thin cord lashed her to the metal guardrail.

Jessica couldn't take it anymore—seeing her sister in pain was too much. Who did these guys think they were? "Hey, what are you doing to my sister?" she burst out.

Jack shot her a glare, tying the rope once more around Elizabeth's wrists.

"Hey, Jack, tie this one *real* tight," Gary called, gesturing toward Jessica.

Jessica sucked in her breath as Jack secured her wrists to the guardrail. She hated these two hijackers. She hated them more than math class. She hated them more than hockey. She even hated them more than black jellybeans.

Finally every single student was tied to the railing.

"This isn't safe, you know," Randy Mason said seriously. "If anything happens to the boat, we'll all be in serious danger. We won't be able to swim free."

"Oh, won't that be a shame," Gary sneered with an ugly smile. "You poor little kids would just have to drown, then, wouldn't you?"

Jessica felt her whole body tense. *I won't think about it, I won't think about it, I won't think about it.*

"So what now, Skipper?" Jack asked.

Gary rubbed a hand over his beard-roughened chin. "Gee, Jack," he said in a goofy voice. "I don't know. Let's see: We've got a boat, we're headed to Mexico, all these pesky kids are taken care of . . . are we forgetting anything?"

"Yeah, Skipper," Jack said. "Two things. Three things, actually." He held up three fingers and counted off. "One, the captain. Two, the other guy. Three, lunch." He looked over to the open deck in the stern of the boat, where ice chests were still sitting open and bits of half-eaten sandwiches were lying around.

"You're right, Jack," Gary continued brightly. "Why don't we have lunch first?"

"Good idea, Skipper," said Jack.

The two thugs made their way to the rear deck and started pawing through the ice chests. Then they settled on benches in the sun, wolfing down the students' lunches and guzzling their sodas.

"Hey, kids!" Gary shouted. "You don't have any beer, do you?" He and Jack laughed uproariously.

"Those stupid jerks," Elizabeth said under her breath to Jessica.

"Yeah," Jessica said angrily. "I hope they choke on those sandwiches."

"This is great, just great," Jerry McAllister mumbled a few feet away, flexing his knee. Already a bruise was forming from where he'd hit the bench.

"You're telling me," Bruce said bitterly. Jessica could see that his knee was badly skinned, and blood was seeping down onto his sandals.

"What are we going to do?" Jessica asked Elizabeth in a low voice. "If no one comes to rescue us, we'll have to rescue ourselves."

"I know." Elizabeth nodded. "Between the two of us, we should come up with something."

Jessica brightened up. "We *are* pretty good at saving each other, huh?"

"Yeah, we are," Elizabeth agreed with a little smile. "Remember when you saved me when I was locked in that building the night of our Psychic Twins exhibition?"

Jessica grinned. "Remember how you saved me when I was in the middle of the JEM cookie disaster?"

"If only one or two of us could get free," Elizabeth whispered. "Then we could try to turn off the boat's engines. I've been working on my knots, but we're all tied pretty tight."

"Well, let's keep thinking," Jessica said, setting her chin with determination. After all, she was Jessica Wakefield. These thugs weren't going to win. They just weren't!

"I'm sorry, Mrs. Wakefield," the coast guard commander said. "We've been hailing the *Island Dreamer*, but she's not responding. And a quick helicopter sweep of the area hasn't turned up anything."

"So what does that mean?" Alice Wakefield asked, her voice rising higher in panic. "Is their radio broken? Why hasn't the captain turned back? Surely the kids have told him that there are no chaperons on board."

The coast guard commander's superior officer came in, and he motioned to the commander. After the boat had left so unexpectedly this morning, Mrs. Wakefield, Mr. Slater, and Mr. Seigel had notified the marina, who had called the coast guard. Since then, they had notified other parents, including Mr. Wakefield and Mrs. Slater, and now they were all in the marina office, trying to decide what to do.

"My name is Captain Robert Burkes," he told the crowd of concerned parents. "I'm afraid we have a troubling situation developing on the *Island Dreamer*. A CB radio operator down by Santa Ana has just picked up a very disturbing mayday call."

Mrs. Wakefield clutched her husband's arm. "A mayday call? Is the boat in trouble?"

Mr. Slater stepped forward. "What's happening with the boat?" he asked in a tense voice. "You have to tell us."

Captain Burkes looked regretful and worried. "It was a mayday call made by a child—someone called Winston."

"That's Winston Egbert," Mr. Seigel said. "But why was he making a mayday call?"

"He said . . . well, I'm afraid he said they'd been hijacked, and were no longer headed to Santa Maria Island."

"Hijacked!" Mr. Wakefield cried, stepping forward. "How could the boat have been hijacked? And by whom?"

"How do we get the boat back?" Mrs. Slater demanded. "Is the coast guard already on its way?"

"Have any of the kids been hurt?" Mrs. Chase asked frantically. "Is my daughter all right?"

"What about Ellen?" Mr. Riteman broke in. "Did Winston mention a girl named Ellen?"

The coast guard officer held up his hand for silence. "The boy said that he didn't know where they were headed, but that they were in trouble," Captain Burkes continued. "Apparently two unknown men have seized control of the boat and disabled the charter captain and crewman. I assume that Winston wouldn't have made the call as a joke, correct?"

Mr. Seigel shook his head. "No, not Winston. Never."

"Then we have to assume that the *Island Dreamer* really is in serious trouble—that it has, in fact, been hijacked." Captain Burkes looked very worried. "The first thing we need to do is determine their location and where they're heading."

"Where are they?" Mrs. Wakefield whispered, her face pale. "Where are my daughters?"

*   *   *

What would Christine Davenport be doing now? Elizabeth wondered, squirming by the guardrail. Christine Davenport was the heroine in books by Amanda Howard, Elizabeth's favorite mystery writer. The teen detective had been in a lot worse scrapes than this and had somehow always managed to get free.

Gently, Elizabeth moved her hands around a tiny bit inside their rope. The rough hemp was scratching her skin. Several kids had slumped to the deck, leaving their hands tied to the rail above them.

There has to be a way out of this, Elizabeth thought, her mind racing. So far she had rejected a million different ideas. Everything depended on their being able to get free of this rope somehow—but how? Winston had a knife, but it was in his pocket, and no one could get to it. What was happening with Captain Moreland? Even though she knew it was probably unrealistic, Elizabeth couldn't help hoping that he was feeling better and was even now sneaking around, putting some great plan into action. *Please, please, be awake and doing something to get us out of this mess,* she pleaded silently.

"OK, kids," Gary said, coming up behind them. "That was a good lunch—thanks. Next time remember that I like extra mayo with my tuna salad, OK?"

Jack snorted with laughter. "Now we gotta take care of the captain and his crewman," he reminded Gary.

"Yeah, that's right," Gary said, rubbing his chin.

"And we gotta take care of them for good."

A chill rushed across Elizabeth, and goose bumps rose on her arms. That didn't mean what she thought it meant, did it? Would Jack and Gary really kill Captain Moreland? She exchanged a fearful glance with Jessica.

"OK," said Gary, glaring menacingly at the kids. "We have to go below for a moment. Don't nobody go nowhere. We'll be right back."

"Oh, geez, what now?" Janet muttered, as the two thugs disappeared into the passenger room. "Anyone got any ideas?"

"Bruce?" Ken Matthews asked. "Do you have any more karate moves up your sleeve?"

"Shut up," Bruce snapped. "I didn't notice you doing anything to help us."

"Bruce is right," Tamara said. "At least he was trying to fight those guys." She shot Ken an irritated glance.

"Look, everyone," Amy said. "There's no point arguing. We know these guys are tougher than us, and they probably have guns. We all have to cooperate and stick together."

"That's true," said Elizabeth, trying to look each of her classmates in the eye. "We have to make a pact: all for one and one for all. OK?"

One by one the field-trippers muttered OK or nodded their heads.

"I just want to go home," Belinda Layton whimpered.

"I know," Elizabeth said firmly. "We all do. But we have to keep calm and try to think of some way out of this."

Just then the two thugs came back out of the passenger room. They were half pushing, half pulling Captain Moreland and Walt Lufkin, who both still looked sick and groggy. They were untied, but they had their hands on top of their heads.

"Looks like you kids got to our friendly neighborhood boat crew, huh?" Gary sneered. "But it didn't do much good, did it? Come on, move it!" he snapped, pushing the captain ahead of him.

Captain Moreland winced as he stumbled across the deck. "Take it easy—we're doing the best that we can."

With a smothered gasp, Elizabeth realized that Gary now held a gun, and he kept jabbing it into Captain Moreland's back. When she looked closely at Jack, she saw he too held a shiny black pistol. Her heart sank even lower, if that was possible. So much for her hopes that Captain Moreland would seize control of the situation.

"On your knees!" Gary barked, nudging the captain and the crewman forward.

"Look, let's talk this out," the captain pleaded. "You can have the boat. But we need—"

"You need to shut up, is what you need," Jack snarled, waving his gun around. "Now, get on your knees!"

Slowly and awkwardly, the two men sank to

their knees on the deck. Looking up, Captain Moreland caught Elizabeth's eye. He looked worried, angry . . . and beaten. She gave him a sympathetic glance, and he looked even more miserable.

"Look, pal," the captain began again. "Do what you want to me and Walt. But it's wrong for these kids to be in the middle of it. Let them go."

"Where?" Jack sneered, turning a winch that unlatched the *Island Dreamer*'s lifeboat. "Let them go into the ocean? Now, there's a thought."

"You know what I mean," Captain Moreland persisted. Sweat ran down his face, and his skin looked sickly and gray. "Stealing a boat is one thing. Kidnapping a bunch of kids is something else."

"Shut up!" Gary barked, kicking the captain in the leg. "They're not your problem anymore." Turning, he nodded to Jack, who lowered the lifeboat over the side of the *Island Dreamer*.

"What are you doing?" Winston demanded. "Why are you lowering the lifeboat? What are you going to do?"

Gary grinned at Winston, a cold, mean grin that showed his crooked teeth. "I'm putting them out of their misery," he hissed.

At gunpoint, the two thugs forced the captain and the crewman into the lifeboat and made them crouch down, still with their hands on their heads. Then Jack lowered the winch the rest of the way, and the lifeboat creaked down to land in the water with a heavy, uneven splash.

"Oh, my gosh, they're setting them adrift," Maria moaned a few feet away from Elizabeth. "Give them some food and water, at least!"

"Ah, I'm so touched," Jack said mockingly. "You're worried they'll get thirsty. Well, I'd be happy to take care of that." With a look of fake concern, Jack went to the stern and pulled a bottle of water from one of the ice chests. Leaning over the rail, he threw it into the lifeboat.

"There you go, me hearties!" he shouted. "Happy trails!" And with a final turn of the winch, he set the lifeboat free.

"I don't believe this," Elizabeth murmured in horror.

"What are we going to do without them?" Jessica whispered anxiously.

"What's going to happen to them, in that little boat?" Amy muttered.

As Elizabeth and the others watched, the lifeboat bounced in the *Island Dreamer*'s wake. The captain and the crewman looked tiny and helpless as the lifeboat drifted away, like a cork in the middle of a vast ocean, with land nowhere in sight.

Elizabeth swallowed hard, meeting Jessica's identical blue-green eyes. Stretching against the rope as hard as she could, she barely managed to touch her sister's hand. Jessica gave her a forced smile.

Elizabeth turned her gaze toward the ocean, where the lifeboat was becoming an ever-smaller blob on the horizon. This was it. The field-trippers were truly on their own now. And she didn't see any way out.

Seven

◇

"What time is it?" Mandy asked wearily.

Todd twisted his wrist inside its rope. "One thirty."

"I'm hungry." Ellen sighed. "I should have eaten my lunch when I had the chance."

Jessica nodded. "I'd die for just a few chips right now."

"You kids shut up!" Gary snarled. He and Jack were in the front of the boat, looking at a map. They had been going in and out of the pilothouse for the past twenty minutes, keeping a close eye on the kids and also doing stuff with the boat: changing course slightly, double-checking their position, using the radio.

Jessica looked out over the water. She was tired of standing, and it was hot in the sun.

"Elizabeth," Jessica whispered. "If you could have anything in the world to eat right now, what would it be?"

Elizabeth furrowed her brow thoughtfully. "Maybe a huge salad at the food court at the mall?" she suggested in a low voice. "Something cool and refreshing. And a huge, tall, icy-cold glass of ginger ale."

"Mmmm," Jessica murmured dreamily. "I think I might have to go for pizza. Two slices with everything on them except anchovies. Extra pepperoni and pineapple. And a root beer. Two root beers." Just thinking about it made her stomach rumble loudly. She didn't think she'd ever been so hungry in her entire life.

"Uh-oh," Elizabeth muttered under her breath. "Look at the sky."

Jessica looked to where her sister was motioning with her head. Far off in the distance, she could see a dark, rolling bank of clouds. She looked down at the waves, and they suddenly seemed to be a bit rougher, topped with white foam, slapping against the side of the boat.

"The storm," she whispered, feeling a new jolt of fear.

Elizabeth nodded. "It looks like it's coming this way," she whispered back.

Several people down the rail, Tamara had started crying softly. "I can't even see the lifeboat anymore," Jessica could hear her whimpering. "They're gone for good. We're not going to make it."

"Shh," Janet said soothingly, though she herself was white and sick-looking with fear. "Come on, Tamara, you're a Unicorn. Unicorns can handle anything, right? We're the best."

Tamara turned tear-filled eyes to Janet. "Janet, the Unicorns are just a school club for girls. We sit around and talk about clothes and boys. It isn't important."

Janet gasped and stared at Tamara, speechless.

"Tamara, you don't mean that," Belinda said, sounding scandalized. "The Unicorns are some of the most important people at Sweet Valley Middle School. Of *course* being a Unicorn will help us get through this."

"That's right." Janet sniffed. "Unicorns don't let a little thing like being hijacked at sea get to them."

Tamara sniffled a little. "OK, OK," she said, her voice cracking.

"Stiff upper lip," Janet said approvingly.

Tamara touched her lip to keep it from quivering.

Jessica chuckled despite herself. "She'll never be president of the Unicorns," she whispered to Elizabeth.

"Too bad," Elizabeth said with a nervous giggle.

Then Gary and Jack clomped heavily down the deck again and disappeared into the pilothouse, shutting the door with a slam. They both looked angry about something.

Sighing, Jessica turned back to the sea. The clouds already seemed bigger, closer, and darker.

Very far off in the distance, she could see gray sheets of rain connecting the clouds with the ocean. It was like a wall of water, and it was getting closer all the time. When the storm hit, would they still be outside here, tied to the railing?

Jessica cast her mind back to that morning. It seemed like a very long time ago. She remembered worrying about what to wear, and how excited she had been about her new bathing suit. Big whoop. *It sure doesn't seem very important now,* she thought, glancing down at her suit. *In fact, worrying about a stupid swimsuit seems kind of—*

Well, kind of childish.

Next to her, Elizabeth sighed.

"What's up?" Jessica asked.

"Oh—nothing." Elizabeth paused. "I was just thinking about this morning," she confessed at last. "How I almost overslept—"

"I wish you had," Jessica said with grim determination. *"I wish we both had."*

"But you woke me up," Elizabeth pointed out. Jessica scowled. *And I wish I hadn't done that!* she told herself. "And then we were almost late for the boat," Elizabeth continued, "because you'd promised all those Unicorns rides—remember?"

"Yeah, I remember," Jessica snapped. "So what?"

"So nothing." Elizabeth stared at her in surprise. "I was just remembering. What's the problem?"

"Well, it sounded like you were blaming me for the whole thing," Jessica said, setting her jaw.

Elizabeth looked blank. "Blaming you? What are you talking about?"

"Oh, forget it!" Jessica wrinkled her nose and looked down at the deck. She felt a surge of her least favorite emotion: guilt. *Maybe if we'd been on time,* she thought, *maybe my mom would be here right now with us. Or maybe we would have found out about the hijackers before we left the dock. Or maybe—*

"I'm not blaming you or anything," Elizabeth protested. Her voice sounded sad. "Really, I'm not, Jess!"

Jessica scuffed the deck with her big toe. She knew that Elizabeth probably didn't really blame her—Elizabeth wasn't like that. But it didn't matter. Because this was one of those terrible, horrible times when Jessica blamed herself.

"Look," Mr. Wakefield said firmly. "If you received a mayday call saying they thought the *Island Dreamer* was headed to Mexico, then we've got to get some boats out there, scouring the area from here to Mexican waters. Plus we need to alert the Mexican authorities."

"We've already alerted the authorities," Captain Burkes reassured him. "But there's a problem with scrambling either boats or planes to look for them at this time."

"What problem?" Mrs. Slater demanded. She was clinging to her husband's arm, her brow wrinkled with worry. "How could there be a problem with looking for our children?"

Captain Burkes pointed to the large weather satellite screen in the coast guard offices. "There's a huge storm coming down the coast from the north, a lot faster than we expected it. It'll be hitting Sweet Valley any minute and continuing down the coast until sometime tomorrow, picking up strength and speed all the time. The weather's just too rough for us to send out boats right now, or helicopters or planes. I'm afraid we'll just have to wait out the storm."

"What does that mean?" Mr. Seigel asked, his voice rising urgently. "If the storm is too rough for search parties, what does it mean for the charter boat?"

Captain Burkes looked very uncomfortable. "If the *Island Dreamer* is caught in the storm," he said reluctantly, "I just don't know . . ."

"Look, dolphins!" Ken Matthews said softly, motioning with his head toward the water. "They must be traveling in a group." For the last several minutes, Jack and Gary had remained in the pilothouse. The students had started to talk among themselves again in low voices.

"Great," Amy said dryly. "We're actually seeing some wildlife on our wildlife field trip. Someone take notes."

Elizabeth watched the three gray fins cutting smoothly through the water. Would they leap out of the water in playful arcs, the way they did at Marine World?

Then Elizabeth blinked. There was something

very undolphinlike about the three gray fins that were following the boat smoothly, keeping up without effort. They stayed in a neat, triangular formation. "Um, guys?" she said shakily. "I don't think those are dolphins. They look to me like"—she swallowed—"shark fins."

Randy examined the fins with a frown. "Elizabeth's right. Those are shark fins. Probably great whites. They're pretty common around here. In fact, more than forty percent of all unprovoked shark attacks along the coast of California have been by great whites."

"Thanks for the information, Randy," Lila said, a thread of hysteria in her voice.

"Oh, you're welcome," he said absentmindedly, still watching the fins.

"Now, shut up," Lila commanded.

Randy looked up, surprised. "I just thought—"

"Do you really think we need a—a biology lesson at a time like this?" she spat out.

Randy looked thoughtful. "Well, I wouldn't say that's a fact of *biology* exactly. It's more—"

"I said shut up!" Lila shrieked.

"Oh." Randy shut his mouth with a snap. "Sorry."

"Listen, you guys," Elizabeth began. "We shouldn't fight with each other at a time like—"

"Psst!" The sound broke into her speech, but she couldn't tell where it came from. She looked around but saw nothing.

"Psst! Elizabeth!"

This time Elizabeth turned around as much as she could. Who was calling her? A glance at the pilothouse showed that the door was still shut, and the hijackers were still inside.

Todd let out a sudden gasp. "Cammi!"

Elizabeth followed his gaze, then sucked in her breath. Cammi Adams was crawling out from beneath a bench! In all the excitement, Elizabeth hadn't even noticed Cammi was missing.

"Cammi, where did you—"

"Shh!" Cammi hissed, interrupting her. She shrank back and watched the pilothouse door for several more moments. The door remained shut. Finally, after what seemed like hours, Cammi crawled out from beneath the bench—and behind her was Donald Zwerdling! Elizabeth stared at them, bewildered. How could she have not noticed that those two hadn't been tied up with the others?

"We were around on the other side of the boat when those guys tied everyone up," Cammi explained in a furtive whisper, anxiously watching the pilothouse door. "I thought they'd never go into the pilothouse!"

"Quick, Donald!" Winston said. "I have a knife in my pocket. Take it out and cut us loose."

"Good idea!" Donald hurried to Winston and dug out the pocketknife. Then he went to work on the rope lashing Winston to the rail.

"I'm next," Bruce demanded, shifting his feet anxiously.

"Then me," Jerry said.

"No, girls first," Lila insisted.

"Unicorns first," Janet said firmly.

Winston was free now and rubbing his wrists where the rope had left raw scrapes on his skin.

"Actually," Cammi said, beckoning Donald, "we've been trying to come up with a plan. And we think we should only cut a couple of people loose."

"What?" Bruce practically yelled.

"Shh!" Cammi hissed at him.

"If only a few of us are loose," Donald explained quietly, cutting at the ropes on Elizabeth's wrists, "the hijackers might not notice, and we could do more damage. If everyone is loose, they'll just pull out their guns and tie us all up again. This is our only chance."

"You're right," Winston said. "Everyone else should stay put and try to cover up our absence."

Jessica frowned. "Excuse me, but if you think I'm standing here with my wrists tied up while you all run free, you're nuts. You get me out of this *now!*"

Elizabeth, finally free from the guardrail, rubbed her wrists, trying to ignore the stinging pain from the rope burns. She gave her a sympathetic look. "Sorry, Jess, but they're probably right. It's better for all of us if you hang tight for a little while longer."

"That's easy for you to say," Jessica said indignantly. "You're cut free."

"You know if everyone was loose, Jack and Gary would just panic and maybe lose their tempers," Elizabeth reasoned. "And they have guns."

"Who's saying everyone should be cut loose?" Jessica asked. "But you can't expect me to stay here with this horrible rope around my wrists." She sighed dramatically. "I just don't how much more I can take. I may even faint!"

"Oh, Jess," Elizabeth began pleadingly.

"If there's anyone here who should be cut free, it's me!" Janet announced. "I'm the president of the Unicorn Club, after all."

"Oh, who gives a hoot?" Bruce broke in scornfully. "Just cut me free, you wimps, and let's get on with it."

"This really isn't helping, you guys," Elizabeth said desperately. "Just sit tight and—" Right then the pilothouse door creaked open. Instantly Cammi and Donald grabbed Winston and Elizabeth and yanked them back through the passenger-house door. Her heart thumping, Elizabeth crouched low and ran as fast as she could to the door marked "Gulls." She and the others crowded in, easing the door shut behind them.

I can't believe that wuss Donald Zwerdling, choosing Winston Egghead over me, Bruce thought furiously as Jack and Gary made their way to the front of the boat. He glanced scornfully at the space on the railing where Winston used to be, and grudgingly eased a little bit closer to Jerry to try to cover up the missing space. But the two hijackers didn't seem that interested in the kids—they went up onto the bow deck with hardly a glance back.

"I'm going to remember this if Elizabeth ever tries to run for class president," Lila whispered angrily to Jessica.

"You and me both," Jessica agreed with a frown. "After all, I'm her very own twin. But does she untie me? No. Instead she runs off with a total stranger, leaving me to fry in the sun."

"Cammi Adams is hardly a total stranger," Maria said dryly. "And their plan does make sense, even if the rest of us are desperate to be loose, too."

"Their plan makes absolutely zero sense," Bruce corrected her. "Obviously, they should have cut some of us guys free before Elizabeth. I mean, what can that wimpy Wakefield girl do to save us?"

Jessica glared at him. "Well, she can't perform any daring karate moves," she said snidely.

"Shut up!" Jerry said.

"At least we tried," Bruce said, narrowing his eyes. "We're not just sitting around waiting to be thrown to the sharks, like some people around here."

"As a matter of fact," Lila said, tossing her hair, "I'm not just waiting around. I'm the daughter of George Fowler, after all. And I'm sure when my dad finds out I've been kidnapped, he'll take charge."

"What do you mean?" Janet asked.

"I mean," Lila said patiently, "that my dad is a very rich man. Of course if I've been kidnapped, he'll call the FBI and the CIA and even the president. Me being in danger is a very big deal. So all we have to do is wait for my dad to rescue us."

"The CIA doesn't have jurisdiction in the United States," Randy Mason pointed out. "Only abroad."

Lila shot him an irritated look. "Whatever. At any rate, I'm sure my dad is offering a huge reward for my safe return. It'll be worth it to the hijackers to take him up on it. And then the rest of you will probably be saved, too."

"Gee, thanks," Amy mumbled.

"Wake up and smell the ocean, Fowler," Bruce said, shaking his head in annoyance. "Your dad probably hasn't even noticed you're missing yet. He's probably on some out-of-town business trip, as usual."

"He is not!" Lila snapped, blushing furiously.

"But *my* folks, on the other hand, are the ones who will be upset," Bruce continued. "I'm the only heir to the Patman millions, after all. It's my folks who have called in the FBI. I bet they've hired real commandos to come rescue me. I bet my parents' reward is about five times as big as yours."

"Is not!" Lila said furiously. "My dad is richer than your whole family put together. My ransom would be ten times as much as yours. Your parents would probably just be glad someone took you off their hands!"

"Would not!" Bruce practically yelled. He couldn't believe how full of herself Lila was. "Everyone knows the Patman fortune is much bigger than anyone else's in Sweet Valley. I bet my ransom would be five million dollars! And my dad could write a check for it!"

"Could not!" Lila screeched. "He'd have to borrow it!"

"Would not!" Bruce shouted back. If his hands hadn't been tied, he would have thrown a soda at Lila. Definitely.

"You guys, keep it down," Ken said urgently.

"You're both being stupid," Janet said with irritation. "Now, be quiet before the hijackers hear you!"

"Too late, little lady," came a sneering voice in back of them. Bruce turned his head to see Gary standing by the door of the passenger room. Gary finished off an icy can of soda, then crumpled the can in his fist and threw it overboard. "I didn't know we had any valuable cargo on board," Gary continued, grinning crookedly.

Bruce felt the color drain from his face. "Valuable cargo? Uh, what do you mean?"

"Cut the innocent act, kid," Gary snapped. He eyed Bruce and Lila. "Yep. You two could come in real useful if we get in a sticky situation. Maybe we'll have to keep you two after all."

"Keep those two?" Todd asked. "What are you going to do with the rest of us?"

"Well, kid, it's like this," Gary said with a fake smile as he came closer. "We just don't need you. A bunch of pesky kids . . . you'll only be in the way. I'm afraid we're going to have to let you go."

"Let us go?" Ken asked. "Where?"

Gary jerked his sandy-haired head toward the water. "Let you go . . . overboard," he said, then he gave an evil, cackling laugh.

"They're going to throw us all overboard," Mandy said a few minutes later, sounding as if she didn't understand what the words meant. Gary had gone back to the pilothouse, and the field-trippers were all staring blankly at one another.

"Maybe he was just bluffing," Bruce said, trying to sound casual. "I mean, maybe if they decide to keep me and Fowler, they might just keep the rest of you, too."

"Maybe not," Tamara said, looking as if she was about to start crying again. "Maybe they're just going to wait for the storm, and then they'll throw us all overboard. And we don't have a lifeboat."

Bruce looked out to the horizon. Already the sky was looking a bit hazy, and the big purple clouds were rolling closer. Now that he noticed it, the boat was rocking more, because the waves were bigger and stronger. The air felt a little bit cooler, and the wind was blowing his hair more. All of a sudden he felt panic rising in his stomach. He didn't care how rich his parents were—let the hijackers ransom Fowler if they wanted. He just wanted to go home and be safe.

"I can't believe it," Maria said, her voice catching a little bit. "We're not ever going home. We'll never see our parents again." Her lip trembled, and Tamara went ahead and burst into tears again.

Oh great, Bruce thought. *That's all we need—a bunch of girls going hysterical.*

"You're all forgetting something," Jessica said firmly.

"Yeah, what's that, Wakefield?" Bruce said snidely, feeling furious with the situation in general and with girls in particular. "Did we all forget that we know how to fly, so that when they throw us overboard, we'll just soar off into the sky?"

"No," Jessica said coolly, her blue-green eyes meeting his blue ones. "You're forgetting that Winston and Cammi and Donald and Elizabeth are all working on a plan to rescue us, right now. And if anyone could pull off a really good plan, Elizabeth could."

Bruce couldn't think of a snappy comeback to that. Strangely enough, it did make him feel a bit better.

Eight

◇

The bathroom marked "Gulls" was tiny and cramped. There was a miniature sink and one toilet with a wooden seat. A small vented window was high on one wall. Cammi and Elizabeth were both sitting on top of the closed toilet seat. Winston was wedged between the sink and the toilet, and Donald leaned against the door, which they had locked.

"Now what?" Elizabeth asked softly.

Cammi shrugged. "We could go over all those plans we thought of again and try to figure out a way to make one of them work."

"I wish we had some kind of poisonous gas that we could flood the pilothouse with," Donald said, keeping his voice low.

"Yeah," said Winston. "Or that we could rig up

some kind of flare or distress signal from stuff we found lying around."

"Well, we can't do any of that," Cammi said, tapping one finger against her chin. "Let's try to focus on what we can do."

"Whatever we do, we better make it soon," Winston said. "That storm is getting closer all the time."

Dropping her head into her hands, Elizabeth stared at the floor, letting her eyes glaze over. Then she started to concentrate as hard as she could. They really had two smaller problems, not just one big problem. For one thing, a huge storm was coming, and they were on a relatively small boat. For another thing, they had to deal with the two horrible hijackers somehow. Her brows knit and her lips pursed. *One problem at a time.* That's what Christine Davenport would say, anyway. A few minutes later, an idea flashed through her head.

She jumped to her feet, and everyone stared at her. "I think I've got it—something that might work."

"Lila," Jessica said softly. "If you had to be shipwrecked on a desert island with either Johnny Buck or Jason Dare, who would you choose?"

Jason Dare was one of the cutest movie stars Jessica could think of. He had been in a commercial with Maria Slater, back when Maria had been a child star.

"Hmm." Lila wrinkled her forehead thoughtfully. On deck, the wind had picked up, and her brown hair was whipping back and forth around her shoulders. Jessica's own hair felt tangled and sticky from the saltwater spray that was misting against the side of the boat. There had been no sign of Gary or Jack lately, and no sign of the four rescuers, either.

"That's a tough one," Lila said. "Johnny Buck is definitely cuter, but Jason Dare is really cute, too, and closer to my age."

"Which one would be better at making fires and fishing and stuff?" Amy asked practically. She had been listening in.

"*Fishing?*" Lila repeated incredulously. "Who cares about fishing?"

"I have to tell you," Maria chimed in, "I'd go for the Buckster. I *know* Jason Dare would be lousy at making fires. He'd probably call his agent to make one for him."

"No phones on a desert island," Jessica pointed out, feeling her spirits lift a little. There was nothing like Johnny Buck to make a girl feel more cheerful. "Just you, the beach, and a hunk. What bathing suit would you be wearing?"

Several feet away, Ken Matthews looked at Todd. "Are girls totally and completely bizarre, or is it me?"

"They're totally bizarre," Todd said.

"I mean, we *are* in a life-or-death situation here, am I right?" Ken asked.

"You're right," Todd said, nodding.

"I mean, we *do* have slightly more important things to talk about, don't we?" Ken persisted.

"We do," Todd agreed.

"We're just trying to keep our minds off things," Jessica said huffily. Honestly! It was like boys *enjoyed* wallowing in gloom, she thought with irritation.

"You're doing a good job of it," Todd acknowledged.

Jessica was about to reply when she noticed their friendly neighborhood sharks were still swimming alongside the boat. The sight of them suddenly made her remember a horrible moment in Booster history. The Boosters had been hired to promote the new food court at the Valley Mall, and she herself had been assigned to wear a totally humiliating hot-dog costume that made her look like a wiener on a bun. Now, with these sharks eagerly circling the *Island Dreamer*, she felt like a wiener on a bun all over again.

She felt her heart flutter in panic. This time she might actually end up eaten.

"Where are Elizabeth and the others?" Mandy asked, her voice tense.

"Yeah, really," Bruce muttered, glaring out at the ocean. "They're sure taking their sweet time. Do they want us to end up as shark bait, or what?"

Shakily, Jessica gripped the guardrail. *I wish he had chosen different words*, she thought miserably.

* * *

Cammi listened carefully at the passenger-room door for several minutes before she made her move. Then, holding her finger to her lips, she dashed out the door, past all her friends, and down the aisle to the stern deck. It took her a moment to find what she needed: Winston's Walkman. Once she found it she stuck it under her shirt, then peered around the corner of the passenger room to make sure the thugs were still nowhere in sight. There was no sign of them. Holding her breath, she dashed back down and leaped through the passenger-room door. Phase One had been accomplished.

"OK," Elizabeth said, huddled again with Winston, Cammi, and Donald in the "Gulls" room. "Everyone knows what to do?"

"Yep," Winston said, nodding.

"Check," Donald said.

"Uh-huh," Cammi said.

"Then let's synchronize watches," Elizabeth said. They all made sure their watches read exactly the same time: two forty-five. "OK, now. I'll head into the galley. Cammi, you and Donald wait behind the door in the captain's quarters. Winston, I'll see you up on top of the pilothouse." She grinned nervously. "I hope."

"I'll be there," Winston promised.

"Then let's move 'em out," Elizabeth said, standing up straight. "Good luck, everybody."

*　　*　　*

The narrow passageway to the boat's galley was dark but short, and Elizabeth made it with no problem. Once inside the galley, she filled up the coffeepot with water and plugged it in, then sat very quietly for three minutes. When the water was hot, she pulled out one of the fold-down seats next to the narrow counter. That would make it easier to climb up onto the counter fast.

Above her the porthole opened.

"Everything OK?" Winston whispered.

Elizabeth nodded. Winston was now sitting on top of the pilothouse. It was party time.

Holding Winston's Walkman, Elizabeth turned it on and spun the dial until she was between stations. Then she cranked the volume up all the way. Loud, scratchy static filled the air.

"Mayday! Mayday!" Elizabeth yelled into the Walkman. "Please help us! We've been hijacked by two guys! This is the *Island Dreamer*! Someone please help us!" Of course, no one was going to hear her plea for help. The Walkman only received radio signals, it didn't send them. But maybe the hijackers wouldn't realize that.

Winston stuck his face through the open porthole. "They're on their way," he whispered excitedly. "Get ready!"

Nodding, Elizabeth jammed the Walkman into her shorts pocket. Moments later, Gary and Jack burst through the galley door, armed with guns.

"What's the big idea, you little punk?" Gary

snarled just as Elizabeth snatched up the coffeepot, yanking the cord out of the wall.

Steeling her nerve, she threw the pot of hot water right at them, spraying their shirts. They yelled and put up their arms. Now was Elizabeth's chance. Swiftly, she leaped up on the counter, catching the edge of the porthole. She started to wiggle through, first one shoulder, then the other. Outside, Winston grabbed her arms and started to help pull her through. She could hear the hijackers screaming and cursing ferociously behind her. Elizabeth wiggled and kicked her way through the narrow window. *Almost home free,* she thought frantically. Then she felt someone grab her foot!

"Oh, no, Win!" she gasped, kicking furiously. "They've got me!"

"Keep kicking!" Winston commanded, crouching down by the porthole.

"I'm trying!" After a few more squirms, Elizabeth was completely through the porthole, except for one foot trapped inside.

But Winston stuck his hand through the porthole and grabbed one of the laces on Elizabeth's sneaker. One quick yank and they came undone. The sneaker fell off into the galley, and Elizabeth snatched her foot free. Then Winston slammed the porthole shut and wedged it into place with a screwdriver he'd taken from the storeroom. Gary and Jack beat against the window, but they were too big to fit through it.

"Let's hurry," Elizabeth said urgently to Winston. "They have guns."

Winston shimmied down the side of the pilot-house, and she slid down after him, her heart pounding. One bare foot hit the deck, and then she was facing all the kids who were still tied to the railing. Winston was right beside her, and he immediately started cutting everyone free.

"Where's Cammi?" Maria asked, just as Cammi and Donald emerged from the passenger room.

"Right here," Cammi said breathlessly, running up to them.

"Did it work?" Elizabeth gasped.

Cammi gave her a big thumbs-up and a grin. "Yep!" she said. "We stuck two broom handles through the lock outside the galley door. Those two thugs are caught like fish in a net!"

"Yay!" Maria cheered, rubbing her wrists, which Winston had just cut loose. "Let's hear it for our rescuers!"

"Hip hip hooray!" Amy shouted, hugging Elizabeth. All down the deck, kids who had been cut free were dancing and leaping around.

"It feels so good to move again," Tamara said, taking big steps up and down the deck.

"I bet we all have scars on our wrists forever," Bruce said bitterly, touching his sore skin.

"But at least we're loose, and the hijackers are trapped," Jerry said happily, stretching his arms over his head.

"The first thing I'm going to do when we get home is sue those two thugs," Bruce said, looking down at his skinned knee. "My dad's lawyers are going to take them for everything they've got."

"You'll have to get in line," Lila declared. "I'm going to sue them first. Kidnapping, mental anguish, et cetera, et cetera. They'll wish they had never heard of this field trip."

"You tell 'em, Li," Jessica said, wiggling impatiently as she waited for her turn to be cut free. "I'm going to wait outside the courthouse when they're on trial and throw eggs at them when they come out."

"Rotten eggs," Aaron elaborated as Winston cut him loose.

Elizabeth grinned. She usually thought it was kind of mean to throw eggs at *anyone*, but she had to admit that in this case—

Crack! Elizabeth jumped as a huge, blue-white bolt of lightning snaked down from the ominous rain clouds. It hit the water not far from the *Island Dreamer*. A thundering drumroll of sound seemed to go right through Elizabeth's chest.

All of a sudden the laughing and dancing and giggling came to a halt. Elizabeth shivered, seeing how close the storm was and how wild it was making the ocean.

"We have to get this boat closer to shore," Donald said, looking up at the sky.

"Who's steering the boat now?" Ken asked, frowning with concern.

"I think it's on automatic pilot," Donald answered, cleaning his glasses on the edge of his shirt. "But I'm not sure. Let's go check it out."

"No, stay up here with me, Lizzie," Jessica pleaded, squirming by the guardrail. Winston was still freeing Lila, who was next to her on the rail.

Elizabeth smiled at her sister. "Sure, Jess." She turned to Donald. "You won't need me, will you?"

"Don't worry, Elizabeth," Cammi answered for him. "What we really need is someone like Bruce." She looked at him innocently. "I mean, since you know how to run a boat like this and everything."

Bruce reddened. "Well, actually, I just think I'll keep an eye on things up here. Make sure Winston can cut the ropes all right and everything."

"Oh, right," Cammi said, rolling her eyes. Then she, Maria, and Donald took off for the pilothouse. They stopped in their tracks as a sound of splintering wood filled the air, coming from the direction of the passenger room.

"I hope those broomsticks are holding," Cammi said nervously. "They were all we could find."

"Quick," Donald said, motioning her forward. "Some of us should lock ourselves in the pilothouse and try to steer toward shore and use the radio."

The three ran off again, and Elizabeth watched as Winston began to cut Jessica free.

"Hurry up, Winston," Jessica pleaded. "Get me out of here."

"I'm trying, I'm trying," he said, sweat dripping

down his brow with the effort. "But my knife isn't very sharp."

Another loud crashing sound shook the boat, then suddenly everyone heard angry bellows of rage coming from the passenger room.

"They've broken free!" Elizabeth gasped. "Hurry, Winston! Get Jessica out of her ropes!"

But it was too late. When Elizabeth turned around, she saw the most awful sight in the world: Gary and Jack bursting through the passenger-room door!

Nine

"Winston!" Jessica yelled. "You come back here!"

But like everyone except Elizabeth, Winston had rushed to hide somewhere on the boat when the thugs burst onto the deck.

"Elizabeth!" Jessica gasped, straining at her ropes. "My hand!" Winston had managed to cut only one hand free—the other was still tied to the guardrail. Frantically Jessica pulled at the knots, but it was impossible to undo them.

Elizabeth, her face white and frozen with fear, began tugging at the ropes, too.

"I won't leave you!" she whispered, her finger-nails scrabbling at the ropes. But Jessica knew that the hijackers would try to get Elizabeth back for helping to lock them in the galley.

Jessica looked at her sister, then at the hijackers

at the other end of the deck. Her heart pounding, she came to a decision. "No, run!" she hissed, pushing at her sister with her one free hand. "They'll try to get back at you for locking them in the galley! Run and hide!"

Elizabeth looked desperately at Jessica's tied hand. "But, Jess—"

"Hurry!" Jessica urged. "I'll be OK!"

After a moment's hesitation, Elizabeth took off down the deck, her one bare foot slapping hard against the wood.

Gary met Jessica's eyes, and she couldn't help shivering. If he had looked fierce before, he looked incredibly horrible now—three times as mean and four times as mad. With a roar of fury, he saw that most of the kids had been set free. Jack, right behind him, started swearing loudly.

"You!" Gary thumped Jack hard in the chest. "Get to the pilothouse and keep this bucket on track! I'll take care of these stupid kids once and for all."

As Jessica watched, her heart in her throat, Gary started after her classmates. *Please, Elizabeth, don't let him catch you,* she pleaded silently. Leaning over, Jessica started to work on her remaining rope with her teeth. It tasted salty and oily, but she bit at it eagerly, feeling some of the frayed edges working themselves loose. *Come on, come on.*

Glancing behind her, Elizabeth saw Gary gaining on her as they raced around the perimeter of the boat. Ocean water was splashing up onto the deck as the waves got higher and higher with every passing minute. The first heavy clouds now totally blocked the sun, though the worst of the storm still looked several miles away.

Rounding the turn in front of the pilothouse, Elizabeth picked up a splinter in her bare foot, but she tried to ignore it. Feet pounding, she skidded against the guardrail and made the turn. Behind her, she heard Gary crash against the pilothouse wall, swear loudly, then start to catch up again.

There's no place to run to, Elizabeth thought, starting to panic. *Nowhere to hide.* Still, she kept running as fast as she could, occasionally seeing other classmates scattering out of her way.

Her breath burning in her throat, Elizabeth rounded the pilothouse again and quickly glanced back. She couldn't see Gary—maybe she had finally outrun him. Now if she could just hide . . .

"Gotcha!"

Elizabeth gasped as a rough hand snaked out from the opposite side of the pilothouse. Too late she realized that Gary had run around to meet her as she turned the corner. Now she was really and truly trapped.

"You little punk!" Gary snarled, putting his face close to Elizabeth's. His big, meaty hand twisted her arm painfully as he pushed her along the deck. "This is all your fault. You've been nothing but trouble, but that's going to end right now."

Ahead Elizabeth could see the guardrail, where only Todd and Mandy were still tied. They both looked as though they were working on the last few knots. *Jessica must have gotten free*, Elizabeth realized with a little burst of hope, as Gary pushed her roughly against the side guardrail.

"Elizabeth!" Mandy bit her lip in consternation as she struggled with the ropes. "Hang on!"

"We'll help you—somehow—" Todd grunted. He yanked his hands as far apart as they would go. "Ugghh!" But the ropes held firm.

"We don't need you kids anyway," Gary grunted. "We should have gotten rid of you a long time ago." He pressed his hip up against Elizabeth's back, pinning her body to the rail.

"Ouch!" Elizabeth drew in her breath. *That hurts!* She tried to squirm around, but Gary's weight against her made it impossible. Worse yet, with her chest pressed hard against the rail, she couldn't even turn her head to see what was happening behind her. *This is so frustrating!* she thought, straining her neck muscles without success. The boat rocked gently in the wind and waves. Elizabeth could see the sky—then the water—then the sky—then the water—then—

Suddenly, Gary ducked down and grabbed her by the legs. *What does he think he's doing?* she wondered, feeling her body rising in the air—higher, higher—

"Thar she blows!" Gary shouted. His powerful arms had her in a viselike grip, and Elizabeth found herself staring down straight into the water. *He's throwing me overboard*, she realized in horror. The whole upper half of her body was sticking out over the rail. "Thar she blows!" she heard again.

Elizabeth sprang into action. Kicking with all her might, she tried hard to land a blow against Gary's stomach. But her feet seemed unable to find their target. "Cut it out, you!" Gary spat out.

Elizabeth tried to spin her body around to face her attacker. She rolled her shoulders first this way, then that. *Hang on!* she told herself, feeling a scream bubble up from her lungs.

"Shut up!" she could hear Gary's voice boom behind her.

Screaming, Elizabeth grabbed at the rail, at Gary's shirt, at anything that could keep her from going into the ocean. The cold, salty spray from the boat's wake splashed up and burned her eyes. She'd managed to turn over, but it didn't seem to have helped much. Her clothes and her hair were getting wetter by the second, and her hands were getting slippery. She remembered the sharks they had seen earlier—how they'd seemed to be swimming alongside the boat. Above her, she caught a glimpse of the cruel glint in Gary's eyes.

"Kiss your short life good-bye," he said mockingly.

Her long blond hair was now trailing in the water below her. *I don't know how much longer I can hold out*, Elizabeth thought, her mind racing frantically. Strength was slipping away from her muscles, just as her own body was slipping away from the boat. There wasn't much more she could do to save herself now.

I don't want to die, she thought.

Jessica, please help me!

As soon as Jessica had bitten through her rope, she had taken off into the passenger room. Through the windows on both sides, she could see one of the hijackers chasing—

Elizabeth.

Jessica sucked in her breath. *I need a plan—and fast!*

She swung around to look at the other kids huddled in the passenger room. *Belinda—Janet—Jerry—Lila—Bruce— Wait a minute.* Jessica rubbed her chin thoughtfully with her index finger. *Say that again.*

"Lila and Bruce," she muttered aloud. A little lightbulb suddenly flashed in her mind. "Lila and Bruce!" she gasped, running in their direction as though shot out of a cannon. "That's it!" *Elizabeth's not the only Wakefield who can make plans*, she thought triumphantly. *She's not the only hero in the family.*

Lila looked up just as Jessica barreled down on her. "Really, Jessica," she began, rolling her eyes.

"Lila!" Jessica cried. "I need your suntan oil, now!"

Lila gave her a scathing glance. "This is hardly the time or the place," she said.

"I'm not going to sunbathe!" Jessica was practically screaming. She dropped her voice a bit, remembering that the hijackers might not be far away. "Hand it over!"

With an elaborate shrug, Lila dug into a side pocket of her bag and pulled out her coconut oil. "Don't waste it," she grumbled. "That stuff's expensive."

Jessica snatched the bottle before Lila could change her mind. Then she turned to Bruce. "Where's your Boogie board?" she demanded, tucking the oil into her shorts pocket.

"Here." Bruce motioned beneath the bench he was sitting on. "Gonna surf back to Sweet Valley?"

Jessica pushed Bruce out of the way and grabbed the Boogie board. Then, taking a deep breath, she headed back out onto the deck, prepared to put her plan into action.

After Jessica left, Bruce sat miserably by the passenger-room door. He could hear other classmates running around, yelling. He could hear Jack banging on the pilothouse door furiously. But somehow it seemed pointless to go out and get caught up in the fray. Not unless he could come up with a sure-fire plan.

I'm helping in my own way, he told himself, nodding his head slowly. *I'm staying out of everyone's way, and I'm helping keep people calm here inside.* He took a quick look around the room. *Yeah,* he thought, nodding a little more firmly this time. *Everyone in here is perfectly calm. Thanks to good ol' Bruce.*

"I bet Donald has already figured out the ship-to-shore radio," he said brightly. *Yeah, Donald knows all about that kind of stuff,* he assured himself. "I could have figured it all out myself, of course," he said with a little laugh. "No problem! But hey, we'll let the kid have his moment of glory." *Good ol' Bruce,* he thought. *Yup, that's me, all right. Always sticking up for the underdog.*

Bruce shifted his glance to Lila. She sat motionless beside him, her eyes glazed, her face pale. "Don't you think so, Lila?" he asked.

Lila stared straight ahead, as though she hadn't heard.

Calm is one thing, Bruce thought with growing irritation. *But you guys are acting like a bunch of zombies!* He elbowed Lila in the ribs. "Lila!"

"Huh?" Lila glared at him.

"Cammi did ask me to go along to the pilothouse, you know," Bruce said proudly. "Of course, I refused. I knew I'd be needed here."

"Uh-huh." Lila looked down at the floor.

"I didn't much mind, not going with them." Bruce shrugged carelessly. "Even though they could have used my help," he said, leaning forward and directing every word into Lila's ear. "I mean, *I* know how to work a ship's radio."

"Do you *mind*!" Lila said, turning away with a grimace. "Go find someone else's ear to spit into."

"Of course, a two-way radio's not exactly a cellular phone," Bruce muttered, gingerly touching the raw scrape on his knee. *What if Donald can't figure it out?*

Next to him, Lila stiffened. "What did you say?"

"I said, a boat's radio isn't exactly a cellular phone," Bruce repeated. "Had your hearing checked lately?"

"Cellular phone," Lila said slowly.

Bruce rolled his eyes. Fowler had obviously cracked. No doubt the men in white coats would be waiting for them on shore when they finally got out of this mess.

If they ever did.

"Oh, my gosh," Lila said softly. Biting her lip, she pulled her bag back over and began rooting through it. A few seconds later, Bruce's eyes bulged as she pulled out—

—a cellular phone.

"I forgot that Daddy lent this to me this morning," she said matter-of-factly. "He does that every now and then, you know. In case of an emergency."

"Well, as soon as an emergency comes up, we'll let you know!" Bruce said, barely able to restrain his anger. "Then maybe you can use it!" *What a dimwit!* he thought. *What a total—*

"The toll charges are pretty steep when you're outside the Sweet Valley city limits," Lila said with a dismissive wave of her hand. "Daddy always says not to use it unless I absolutely have to."

Bruce rolled his eyes. It was all he could do not to reach out and strangle her with his bare hands. *Of all the stupid, idiotic, lamebrained*—Bruce ran out of adjectives. "We could have been out of this mess three hours ago," he remarked, glaring at Lila.

"Well, maybe if you'd mentioned cellular phones *before*," Lila retorted. Quickly, she turned the phone on as the other kids gathered around. "Hmm, the signal's fuzzy." She went to stand close to the open passenger-room door. Bruce followed and watched as she punched in a series of numbers.

"Are you calling the police?" Belinda asked, hovering close by.

"My dad," Lila said. "Oh, wait—I got the machine."

"Your dad!" Bruce shrieked, scarcely able to believe his ears. *Who does she think she is, anyway?* "Give me that!" He grabbed the phone out of Lila's hand. He clicked the button to clear it and dialed 911.

"Yes?" a voice answered. "Is this an emergency?"

"*Some* people think so," Bruce said through clenched teeth. "Listen, this is the *Island Dreamer*, a charter boat out of Sweet Valley. We've been hijacked by two thugs, and we're on our way to Mexico. A storm's coming, and you've got to get us off this boat."

"You're saying you've been hijacked?" the operator asked with surprise.

"Of course that's what I'm saying!" Bruce yelled. "By two guys who robbed a bank this morning in Sweet Valley. Now, get us off this boat!" *Honestly, where do our tax dollars go?*

"Where are you now?" the voice asked.

"How should I know?" Bruce demanded. "That's part of your job, isn't it? They say we're on our way to Mexico, and we've been cruising pretty fast since eight o'clock this morning. But who cares? Just come and get us!"

Next to him, Lila was trying to grab the phone back. "Call my father!" she yelled, clutching the receiver. "Mr. Fowler of Fowler Enterprises in Sweet Valley!"

"Knock it off!" Bruce hissed. He held the phone high out of her reach.

"It's my phone!" Lila cried, jumping up and trying to get it back.

"I beg your pardon?" The operator's voice crackled through the receiver.

"You're being too stupid about it!" Bruce hissed to Lila, whirling around so she couldn't reach the phone. "Send the coast guard!" he yelled into the phone. "The army, the navy, somebody!" Lila grabbed the phone once more and Bruce gave her a swift kick in the shin.

"Aieee!" Lila shrieked.

"Is this a genuine emergency?" The operator sounded annoyed. "If you're just a bunch of kids playing around, please clear the line. There are genuine emergencies out there and—"

Kids playing around? Fury welled up inside Bruce. *Of all the nerve!* "The ocean's getting rougher!" he cried, realizing that the boat was pitching back and forth in the increasingly large waves. "You've got to help us!"

With a final grab, Lila snatched back her phone. "Call my father!" she said. "Mr. Fowler of Fowler

Industries! That's F-O-W-L-E-R! He'll know what to do!"

"Quit wasting time!" Bruce shouted, trying to snatch the phone back. But Lila flung out her arm to keep it out of reach . . . and all at once the phone slipped out of her hand, sailed through the air, and disappeared over the side of the boat into the water below.

Bruce stared at Lila, and she stared back at him, her brown eyes wide and mortified. She covered her mouth with her hand, and fat tears welled up in her eyes.

"I don't believe this," he began. "I do not believe this!" He compressed his mouth into a fine line as he tried to think of the absolute worst insults he had ever known. "You are the most—"

But abruptly Bruce shut his mouth and looked away. *A bunch of kids playing around*, he thought sadly. Somehow, he realized, yelling at Lila wouldn't help. Feeling numb, he turned and went to sit on a bench. He didn't want to look at anyone or talk to anyone.

They'd had a chance for rescue, and now it was gone.

And there was nothing anyone could do about it.

Ten

◇

OK, Jessica, it's now or never.

Taking a deep breath, Jessica sneaked up behind Gary. *Good.* She could see that Elizabeth still had her knees hooked over the guardrail. *Hang on, hang on,* she begged. *Just a few more seconds—if all goes right!*

Jessica crept steadily forward. Twelve feet—ten feet—five. Close enough. She gulped, watching her sister struggle with the robber. Then she shook her head firmly.

Enough watching. Time for action!

Careful to be as quiet as possible, Jessica sprayed a puddle of suntan oil right behind Gary's feet. He was too busy trying to unhook Elizabeth's fingers from his shirt to notice.

"Let go, punk!" he growled. "Face it—you're going to be lunch for the sharks." He pried one finger loose—then two—"Time to say your prayers!"

"I don't think so, you stupid jerk!" Jessica yelled right behind him, trying hard to attract his attention. Thinking fast, she aimed the bottle of suntan oil and squeezed with all her might. A coconutty stream arced through the air, hitting Gary on the back of his neck. It began to drip down his shirt collar.

With a low growl, Gary swung around to see Jessica. He had a furious expression on his face.

"Back off, kid!" he shouted. "Or you'll be next!"

One of his hands rose menacingly toward Jessica's face. Jessica's heart was thundering, but she knew she couldn't stop now. Behind him she could see Elizabeth's hand grope for the top of the railing. *Keep him looking this way,* she thought frantically. She did her best to choke down her fear. *Get him to come toward you,* she commanded herself.

Aiming her bottle again, she sprayed Gary in the face. "You stupid kid!" he bellowed with rage. He lunged toward her . . . and in the next instant put his foot down hard in the puddle of oil on the slick wooden deck.

Wham! His face twisted in horrified surprise, Gary went down hard, slamming his back against the deck. His mouth gaped like a fish as he tried to get his breath. *Yes!* Jessica moved in for the kill.

She grabbed Bruce's Boogie board and raised it high above her head. Trying her best not to think about what she was doing, she brought it down with all her might on Gary's skull. *Please,* she begged, *let once be enough!*

There was a dull *thunk!* His eyes rolled to the back of his head and he slumped down. He was out cold. Breathing hard, Jessica ran to the side of the boat. Elizabeth's face had just appeared over the guardrail. She looked white as a ghost. Jessica grabbed her sister's hands and yanked her up with all her might.

"Oh, Jessica!" Elizabeth breathed, as Jessica pulled her over. They hugged each other tightly. "You saved my life!"

"Of course I did," Jessica said, feeling Elizabeth wet and shivering against her. Her heart pounded as she realized how close she'd come to losing her sister. "I had to. You're—you're my only twin." Her voice failed her, and she caught Elizabeth up in the biggest of bear hugs.

"I know." Elizabeth clutched her tighter.

"Oh, Lizzie—" Tears welled in Jessica's eyes.

"What is it?" Elizabeth asked shakily.

Jessica's words came out in shuddering sobs. "I'm—so glad—you're safe."

"Way to go, Jessica!" *Todd's voice,* Elizabeth thought, turning toward him and letting go of her sister at last. *Good. Somehow he's gotten free.* Behind him came several other kids. She shivered. *If it hadn't been for Jessica,* she thought, biting her lip, *I might never have seen any of them—ever again.*

"Are you all right?" Todd asked, coming up to her. He looked at her with concern.

"I am now, thanks to Jessica," Elizabeth said.

"Is he dead?" Mandy whispered, glancing down at Gary, her hand to her throat.

"No," Ken said, bending over him. "He's still breathing. But we've got to get him tied up before he comes to." He and Todd quickly began gathering the pieces of rope that had tied all the kids to the guardrail.

"Ten feet should be enough," Elizabeth decided. She still felt a little woozy from her trip halfway over the side of the *Island Dreamer.* She reached out to tie a knot but gave it up after a moment. Her fingers couldn't quite be trusted, she realized. She let the others tie Gary's hands and feet together instead, just as Lila, Bruce, and the others joined them from the passenger room.

Bruce stood guard with the Boogie board. "If he opens his eyes, I'll just give him another whack," he said, looking at Gary with disgust.

Todd lashed the thug's hands together tightly. "He's just lucky nothing happened to Elizabeth."

"*I'm* lucky Jessica was here," Elizabeth said, smiling at her sister. Bending over, she gingerly took Gary's gun out of his belt. Swiftly, she threw it overboard into the ocean.

"Hey, we might have needed that," Bruce objected.

Elizabeth shook her head firmly. "No—none of us could have used it. But he could have used it on us."

"Elizabeth's right," Jessica said. "It's much better off where it is." She glanced happily at Elizabeth. "Oh, Lizzie, she said, it looks like maybe we're safe at last!"

Elizabeth grinned back. "Safe," she said dreamily. "I like the sound of that word."

Suddenly, almost as if in response, a gust of wind blew through Elizabeth's hair. Elizabeth could hear the passenger-room door bang against its hinges. She cast an anxious glance toward Jessica.

Jessica looked as nervous as she did. "Um, what were we saying about being safe?" she asked weakly.

Elizabeth squeezed her hand and looked out at the violent sea. No doubt about it: The storm was almost upon them.

"Where's Jack?" Elizabeth asked anxiously a moment later. The approaching storm made her realize that she still had a bunch of reasons to be nervous.

"Outside the pilothouse," Winston told her. "I think."

Elizabeth nodded. "All right. Let's go."

"Be careful," Jessica whispered. "We don't know where Jack's gun is."

Elizabeth was too busy making her way over the rolling deck to answer. In front of her someone was yelling, and there was another noise, too: a noise that sounded vaguely like a fist hammering on a door. *Jack.* She drew in her breath.

Suddenly Winston stopped in his tracks. He snapped his fingers as if he had just thought of something.

"What's up?" Elizabeth asked curiously. She stared in the direction he was pointing. Attached to the wall ahead she could see a thick Styrofoam life preserver ring, with *Island Dreamer* painted on it.

"I'm going up on the roof of the pilothouse," Winston whispered to Elizabeth. "When I get up there, throw me the ring."

"OK," she whispered.

"Then you and Jessica get Jack close to the wall," Winston instructed. "Try to get him right beneath me, if you can."

Why not? Elizabeth thought. *It's worth a try.* She nodded. Quickly Winston climbed on a bench, then grabbed hold of some ropes and handholds. In no time he was slithering up onto the roof of the pilothouse. Elizabeth quietly unhooked the life preserver and handed it up to him. The boat was heaving back and forth among the waves now, and as Winston crawled into position, a chilly gray rain began to fall.

"Do you know what we have to do?" Elizabeth asked Jessica, swallowing hard.

"I think so." With Todd, Ken, Belinda, and Lila behind them, they rounded the corner of the pilothouse. *Ugh!* Elizabeth recoiled as she saw Jack, his black hair stringy in the rain, pounding frantically on the door. Elizabeth held her breath, certain the door could never hold firm against his blows.

"Let me in, you little creeps!" he shouted over the roar of the wind. 'Or I'm going to come in shooting!"

"Go away!" Cammi screamed from inside. "We've

called the coast guard, and they're on their way! You might as well give up!"

"Forget it!" Jack yelled back. "I'm going to shoot the lock off, and then all of you are going overboard! Gary just threw one of your friends over! How do you like that?"

Elizabeth gasped and started forward. It was all she could do not to blurt out the truth: that no one had been thrown overboard and that Gary was lying unconscious on the deck right now. *Quiet, quiet,* Elizabeth commanded herself, knowing that they could only defeat Jack if they could take him by surprise. *Let him think he's winning.* Digging her heels firmly into the deck, she settled back into place.

She motioned silently to Jessica, pointing to Jack's gun, which was tucked into the back of his waistband.

"Now I'm going to count to three," Jack warned. "If you know what's good for you, you'll stand away from the door. One!"

Elizabeth couldn't wait any longer. "If *you* know what's good for *you*," she said loudly, her hands on her hips, "you'll go take a look at what happened to your friend."

"Two!" Jack whirled around and glowered at Elizabeth. He took a step forward. "Hey—wait a minute." He reached back for the gun. "Gary just threw you overboard."

"That's what *you* think!" Jessica taunted him, standing up. "Your partner might have been too

strong for Elizabeth, but I was too smart for him.
Jessica one—hijackers nothing!"

"Back off, kid," Jack snarled. "I'm warning you."

"No," Jessica yelled. "*We're* warning *you*. Don't
take a step closer to the pilothouse."

Good one, Jessica, Elizabeth thought approvingly.
Some of her Unicorn deviousness could really pay
off. *The pilothouse was right where Winston was waiting for him.*

"Yeah?" Jack sneered. "What are you going to
do to me?" Mockingly, he stepped a little closer
to the pilothouse, as if daring them to take action. It was all Elizabeth could do not to look up
at Winston.

"Maybe we'll do the same thing to you as we
did to Gary," Todd said angrily, crossing his arms
over his chest.

"Yeah," Ken added in a taunting voice. "He's
not in good shape right now."

Jack frowned. "What are you talking about?" He
raised his head. "Gary! What are these kids up to?"
But he got no answer. The wind seemed to snatch
the words right out of his mouth.

Elizabeth brushed her wet hair out of her face. The
rain was stinging by now, and the boat rocked wildly.
"We told you," she said, desperate to put Winston's
plan into action. "We took care of him. Now you better stay away from the pilothouse—or else."

An angry glint shone in Jack's eyes. Curling his
lip, he took another step closer to the door. He

thrust his chest forward. "Or what, huh?" he mocked. "You'll do what?"

"This!" Winston yelled, throwing the life preserver down with careful aim.

All right! Elizabeth pumped her fist in the air as the ring slid swiftly and firmly over Jack's head and shoulders. "What?" he said, bewildered. He began to thrash about, but Elizabeth was too quick for him. Dashing forward, she yanked it down over his arms.

"Get this thing off me!" Jack bellowed, shaking his huge body back and forth. He scratched and clawed at the ring. "I'll get you!" he swore. "So help me, I'll—!"

"Bruce, quick!" Lila screamed, cupping her hands around her mouth. "Hurry!"

If I can just hold on, Elizabeth thought. The Styrofoam ring, slippery with rain, was beginning to slide out of her grasp. She pulled harder on the life preserver. "Bruce!"

"Hai-yah!" Bruce ran up with his Boogie board. Jumping into the air, he cracked it down on Jack's head.

Jack looked stunned for a moment. He staggered, then slowly sank to his knees. As Elizabeth watched fearfully, Jack's eyes rolled back into his head and he pitched forward, propped up a little by the life preserver ring.

"Nice shot!" Lila said to Bruce.

Bruce grinned proudly. "Of course," he said nonchalantly. "Anytime you need anyone to do a few surefire karate moves, just call on me."

"Sure thing," Elizabeth said quickly, deciding not to waste time arguing with him. "Hurry, we have to tie him up," she instructed, pitching Jack's gun overboard. "Be careful—the deck's slippery." An icy wave washed over the boat's bow, and Elizabeth realized her teeth were chattering. *I wish I had warm, dry clothes to change into!* she thought, as Todd, Ken, Bruce, and Lila started to drag Jack down the aisle to be tied up.

Jessica was already knocking on the pilot-house door.

"Everyone can come out now!" she yelled. "It's safe! Both hijackers are out cold!"

The door opened immediately, and Donald Zwerdling poked his head out. "Really?" he asked, looking around. "The two thugs have been neutralized?"

Jessica nodded proudly as another icy wave washed over her sneakers. "Yep. So what's going on in there? Have you been steering the boat toward shore? Did you get the radio to work? Did you guys really call the coast guard?"

Donald frowned as a mist of seawater sprayed up and fogged his glasses. He took them off and tried to dry them on his shirt.

"I'm afraid—" he began, shaking his head. "I'm afraid we have some bad news about that."

Eleven

◇

"What do you mean, the sea charts are useless?" Lila demanded.

Donald pushed his glasses up his nose. "Just what I said." His tone was flat, and his voice slow and serious. "We're so far from Sweet Valley that our location isn't on any of the charts in the pilothouse." He looked around the passenger room, where the whole group was gathered. "Um—I'm sorry."

Jessica felt her heart beginning to thump. *If the sea charts are useless*, she thought, *then—*

Then how are we going to get home?

"Doesn't this tub have a satellite tracking system?" Bruce asked. He coughed. "Like I have on *my* boat."

Donald's expression didn't change. "No satellite tracking system. Sorry."

Cammi stood up next to Donald. "Also, the radio didn't really work that well. One of the stupid hijackers had left a cup of coffee on the dashboard, and when the boat tipped a little, the coffee spilled into the radio." Jessica leaned forward to hear what she was saying over the roar of the wind. "So it worked for about two seconds when we tried to send a distress signal," Cammi continued, "but then it conked out."

"I can't believe this is happening!" Lila groaned, burying her face in her hands.

Janet stared straight ahead of her, as though in a trance. "What did I ever do to deserve this?"

Jessica stole a quick glance around the room. *Everyone looks terrible*, she thought. All the kids were waterlogged and practically blue with cold. Shivering, she wished she'd worn something a little more substantial than a swimsuit and T-shirt.

"OK," Winston said seriously. "We have to decide what to do now. Any suggestions?"

Tamara raised her hand.

"Yes?" Winston said from where he stood on a bench at the front of the room.

"Does anyone have any motion-sickness pills?" Tamara asked in a weak voice.

Looking over at her, Jessica saw that Tamara was a pale shade of green. And she wasn't the only one. In fact, the boat was tossing about on the waves so much that it was a miracle everyone wasn't sick as a dog.

"Actually, I have some," Lila said, digging in her

bag. She brought out a box and passed it to Tamara. "Everyone who needs one, help themselves."

"Is there anything you *don't* have in that bag?" Bruce asked in disbelief. "Like, do you have the *coast guard* in there?"

Lila made a face at him and zipped her bag shut.

The boat pitched again. Jessica slid off her bench and almost landed on top of Gary, who was lying like a lumpy sack of grain on the floor. *Yuck!* She scrambled back up again. She knew that the hijackers were tied up, but she didn't want to be anywhere near them.

"So, in summary—" Donald began when no one else said anything.

"In summary, we're up a creek," Bruce said flatly. He shook his head. "Man, oh, man. This really bites."

The boat rolled the other way, and Jessica slid closer to her sister. It was getting harder and harder to balance. Looking out the window, Jessica could see that the sky was completely black and purple with awful, heavy clouds. It was raining very hard, and the waves were huge and white-crested. A smooth, gray-green wall of water crashed over the side of the boat.

"In essence, Bruce is correct," Donald confirmed. "I'm afraid we have very few options at this point."

"No radio, no lifeboat—what are we going to do?" Belinda asked fearfully.

"There are life jackets in the storeroom," Maria

said firmly, standing up and opening its door. "I'm not sure if there's enough for everyone, but let's start passing them out. Weakest swimmers first." She pulled out a huge tangle of musty-smelling orange life jackets.

Jessica started forward, only to fall into Ken when another wall of water washed over the decks.

"Ooof!" Ken said, pitching forward. He glared over his shoulder at Jessica. "Why don't you watch where you're going, huh?"

"Sorry," Jessica began, when Cammi lurched into her from the other side.

"One at a time!" Maria yelled, trying desperately to keep her own balance.

"I'm sure my dad knows where we are," Lila said frantically to no one in particular. "I'm sure he's on his way. Probably in the company helicopter." She looked down at the floor. "He wouldn't forget about me. I—I know he wouldn't."

Jessica nodded. "I know, Lila."

"The helicopter can beat a storm like this," Lila continued, taking a deep breath. "And my dad's strong and smart and everything. He'll—he'll be here soon." She swallowed hard.

Jessica met Elizabeth's eyes. "What do you think's going to happen?" she asked softly.

Elizabeth bit her lip. "I don't know," she said in a low voice. "We're in a pretty tough spot. But if the boat holds together, maybe it won't be too bad."

Jessica shuddered. "Even if the boat holds together,

we still don't have any food," she reminded her. "Most of the ice chests have been washed overboard by now."

"We can live without food for a while," Elizabeth said. "We'll just have to stick together and make the best of it."

Jessica wished she could share her sister's determination. *No food, no charts, no satellite tracking equipment*, she thought dismally as she made her way over to the life-jacket pile. *No radio. No rescuers—*

No hope.

At that moment, the biggest wave yet crashed against the side of the small charter boat. A huge, bone-crunching jolt knocked Jessica off her feet. For a moment a terrible whining, crashing sound seemed to surround her. The boat lurched and spun to the left. Jessica heard a scream, and then another and another. . . . Bruce grabbed a bench to try to stay upright. Donald fell back against a wall. Jessica caught her breath. *Why aren't we tipping back up again?* she wondered fearfully, struggling to her knees.

Next to her, Mandy gripped her arm for support. "I was—I was in a carnival funhouse once— that tipped over like this," she said breathlessly. "It was fun then. It isn't—so much fun—now."

"What's going on?" Jessica asked Winston, who was on her other side.

Winston met her eyes. "I think we must have hit something and sprung a leak somewhere," he said quietly. "If we're taking on water, the boat is only going to keep tipping over. And then . . ."

And then we'll sink, Jessica realized. *The boat will sink, and we'll all drown.*

Suddenly, Tamara began to scream. "I can't stay in here!" she cried, her eyes wild. "We're all going to be trapped inside! Let me out, let me out, *let me out!*" Grabbing on to benches and pipes and anything else she could find, Tamara frantically made her way to the passenger-room door. But as soon as she unlatched it, the wind flung it open and slammed it hard against the wall.

"Tamara, no!" Jessica shouted, trying to follow her. "Stop her, someone!"

Todd and Ken tried to go after her, but Elizabeth was closest. Just as she was reaching out to grab Tamara's jacket, the panic-stricken girl lurched through the door onto the deck.

"Elizabeth!" Jessica shouted, running forward as fast as she could across the tilted floor. Her heart was in her mouth. "Elizabeth!"

But it was too late. Elizabeth had disappeared from sight.

Out on the deck, the storm seemed twenty times worse. Pouring rain lashed Elizabeth's face so hard she could barely open her eyes, and the wind nearly blew her off her feet. Through the stormy darkness, Elizabeth could dimly see Tamara trying to claw off her life jacket.

"Tamara!" Elizabeth reached out for her, but

the wind knocked them both back against an out-side wall.

"I'll never make it home!" Tamara wailed, grab-bing on to a pipe that stuck out from the wall where she stood. "I'll never see anyone again!"

"Yes, you will!" Elizabeth swallowed hard, not sure if she could believe her own words. Slowly she started to make her way over to Tamara. "You're safer inside," she yelled, hoping that the pipe was firmly attached to the wall. *If it breaks—* She didn't want to think about it. "Come back inside!" *If I can just convince Tamara to come a little closer . . .*

"You can do it, Tamara!" Todd was standing at the open doorway, one hand firmly braced against the frame, the other reaching out to Elizabeth. Tamara was clutching the pipe with all her might and crying, her tears whipped from her face by the wind and the rain. Elizabeth crept a little closer to Tamara and stretched out her hand.

"Come back inside, Tamara!" she shouted over the storm. "Come back inside!"

"It's warm and dry in here!" *That was Winston,* Elizabeth guessed, not daring to turn around.

She met Tamara's frightened eyes. "Come back," she said, forcing a grin onto her face. "We'll—um, we'll start a fire and roast marshmallows, and sing songs." She knew that there weren't any marshmal-lows on the boat, but she wanted to lure her with activities that sounded warm and toasty. "And, um, maybe Lila has some hot chocolate in her bag—"

"Really?" Tamara choked back a sob and fixed Elizabeth with a frightened gaze. "Hot chocolate?"

"I'm almost sure," Elizabeth lied, shivering in the driving rain. *Anything to get her inside*, she thought, crawling a couple of feet closer. *Anything to—*

Just then, an enormous ten-foot wave crashed over the boat. Elizabeth fell against the wall. Then, to her horror, she felt the wave sweeping her body powerfully forward—toward the ocean.

Stunned and spitting out salt water, Elizabeth grabbed for the rail. Somewhere in the distance, she could hear Jessica screaming her name. Then another wave blanketed the boat, knocking Elizabeth to the deck. This time she got water in her nose and mouth. She felt herself beginning to choke.

"Elizabeth!" Todd screamed. "Hang on!"

I'm trying! One of Elizabeth's hands, slick with water and numbed by the cold, closed around the guardrail. Elizabeth opened her eyes—only to see a third wave bearing directly down onto her head.

Help! Elizabeth struggled to hang on, but her grip couldn't withstand the powerful wave. She arched her back in an effort to save herself from going overboard. Her arms flew out, and her mouth opened in a silent cry. *The guardrail!* she thought, panicked. *The guardrail!* Was she above it or below it?

Where is the boat? Elizabeth's heart pounded. Suddenly there was nothing around her, nothing but water—and the steady, ominous beating of the waves against the side of the *Island Dreamer. I'm in the ocean*, she realized, struggling to keep calm.

In the ocean, in the middle of a storm!

"Elizabeth!" Jessica and Todd were shouting, but by now their voices were nothing but thin, far-away ribbons of sound.

The water was freezing, Elizabeth realized vaguely, and the waves were unbelievably huge. She felt like a very small cork being tossed from one enormous swell to the next. Already the *Island Dreamer* looked far away, almost like a small white toy boat being sunk in a bathtub.

A wave washed over her head, and Elizabeth swallowed a mouthful of salt water. It made her feel sick, and her body was going numb from the frigid water. *I've got to get back to the boat*, she thought, kicking her legs and waving her arms to keep afloat. But another wave swept her farther out to sea, and the boat looked even smaller and more impossible to get to.

I've got to make it, Elizabeth thought, a thread of panic rising in her stomach. *I've got to get back to Jessica.* A ferocious swell of water swept over her head, and for terrifying moments she was sucked beneath the waves into the icy black ocean. Paddling furiously, she broke the surface again and gasped for breath. She couldn't keep this up much longer, she realized. It was still raining, and the ocean waves were tugging her ever downward and out to sea. Already her arms and legs were aching and tired, useless against the strength of the ocean.

I've got to make it, she thought wearily as she sank underwater again. *I've got to make it*. This time when she bobbed back to the surface, she could barely keep her eyes open. Her arms and legs felt like lead, and she was no longer cold. The waves were tossing her around, but if she just relaxed, it didn't seem so bad. Suddenly getting back to the boat seemed like too huge an effort. She was OK where she was. Sleepily she blinked; she could no longer see the boat anyway, no longer hear anyone calling her. Well, that was OK. Everything was OK. She was very, very tired, and had to just close her eyes for a minute. . . .

The next time a wave washed over Elizabeth's head, spreading her long blond hair around her like a golden sunburst, she didn't struggle. There, in the darkness of the ocean storm, she gave up the fight.

What will happen to Elizabeth and her classmates on the Island Dreamer? *Read Sweet Valley Twins 92,* ESCAPE FROM TERROR ISLAND, *the exciting conclusion of the Nightmare at Sea miniseries, to find out.*

We hope you enjoyed reading this book. If you would like to receive further information about available titles in the Bantam series, just write to the address below, with your name and address:

Kim Prior
Bantam Books
61–63 Uxbridge Road
Ealing
London W5 5SA.

If you live in Australia or New Zealand and would like more information about the series, please write to:

Sally Porter
Transworld Publishers
(Australia) Pty Ltd
15–25 Helles Avenue
Moorebank
NSW 2170
AUSTRALIA

Kiri Martin
Transworld Publishers (NZ) Ltd
3 William Pickering Drive
Albany
Auckland
NEW ZEALAND

Hang out with the coolest kids around!

THE UNICORN CLUB

Jessica and Elizabeth Wakefield are just two of the terrific members of The Unicorn Club you've met in *Sweet Valley Twins* books. Now get to know some of their friends even better!

A sensational new *Sweet Valley* series.

1. SAVE THE UNICORNS!
2. MARIA'S MOVIE COMEBACK
3. THE BEST FRIEND GAME
4. LILA'S LITTLE SISTER
5. UNICORNS IN LOVE
SUPER EDITION: UNICORNS AT WAR
7. TOO CLOSE FOR COMFORT